GRAND & HUMBLE

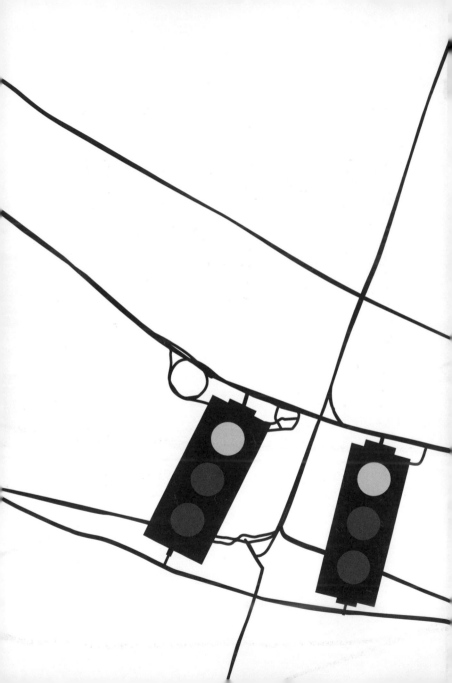

BRENT HARTINGER

GRAND & HUMBLE

HarperTempest
An *Imprint of* HarperCollins*Publishers*

HarperTempest is an imprint of HarperCollins Publishers.

Grand & Humble
Copyright © 2006 by Brent Hartinger

www.harperteen.com

Library of Congress Cataloging-in-Publication Data
Hartinger, Brent.
    Grand & Humble / Brent Hartinger.— 1st ed.
        p.   cm.
    Summary: Alternating chapters follow the lives of two high school boys, whose recent nightmares and premonitions of disaster are linked to mysterious past events.
    ISBN-10: 0-06-056727-9 (trade bdg.) — ISBN-13: 978-0-06-056727-9 (trade bdg.)
    ISBN-10: 0-06-056728-7 (lib. bdg.) — ISBN-13: 978-0-06-056728-6 (lib. bdg.)
    [1. Memory—Fiction. 2. Space and time—Fiction.] I. Title: Grand and Humble. II. Title.
PZ7.H2635Gra 2006   2005005505
[Fic]—dc22   CIP
                                                                           AC

Typography by Christopher Stengel
1 2 3 4 5 6 7 8 9 10
❖
First Edition

For Michael Jensen,
who is both grand and humble

And for Steve Fraser,
who is just grand

GRAND & HUMBLE

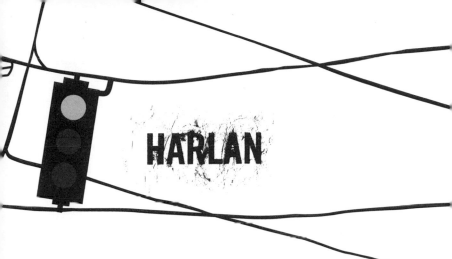

HARLAN

Two faces. Two sides to the same person. That's what Harlan's English teacher was getting at. It was so obvious, he couldn't believe everyone else hadn't seen it right from the start. How could they be so blind?

"Harlan?" Mrs. Woodburn said to him from up near the blackboard. "Perhaps you'd like to enlighten the class with your opinion on the subject at hand."

"My opinion?" Harlan said, with the perfect drawl.

"Yes, your *opinion*."

He grinned. "My opinion is that blue is a really good color on you. It goes with your eyes."

There was a moment's silence, like the instant after you slam the gas pedal, but before the spark plugs fire and the tires squeal out.

Then they squealed. All at once, the class started laughing, just like Harlan had known they would.

And Mrs. Woodburn blushed. Harlan had known she'd do that too.

But Mrs. Woodburn was more self-possessed than he'd thought. "Thank you so very much, Harlan," the teacher said, trying to keep her voice even. "I'll keep your opinion in mind when I'm dressing each morning. But I'm wondering if you have an opinion on the subject of *The Scarlet Letter*."

"Oh," Harlan said. "*That* subject at hand." The class snickered again, if only at the boldness of his banter.

"Harlan, just answer the question!" Mrs. Woodburn was getting impatient. It was, therefore, time to get serious. The difference between Harlan and the idiots who spent their afternoons in detention was that he always knew not to push things too far.

"Split personality," he said without missing a beat.

Mrs. Woodburn hesitated. "What about it?"

"That's my opinion. That's what you're getting at. It's like the characters have two different sides to themselves. Opposite faces."

"Which characters?"

"Hester, Chillingworth, Dimmesdale," Harlan said. "Pearl too, in a way. They all have public personas that are at odds with their private ones. And the challenge they have in *The Scarlet Letter* is whether or not they can reconcile the two conflicting natures in their souls. The characters who do—Hester, Dimmesdale, and Pearl—find peace. The character who can't—Chillingworth—doesn't. According to the author, he shrivels away 'like an uprooted weed that lies wilting in the sun.'"

Mrs. Woodburn stared at him. He'd struck her speechless, and he'd intended that too. Just because he was popular and athletic and good-looking, that didn't mean he wasn't smart. Why was that always so hard for people to remember?

"Thank you, Harlan," Mrs. Woodburn said simply.

Harlan leaned back in his chair and stretched his legs out under his desk. Mrs. Woodburn wouldn't be calling on him again anytime soon.

"Hel-looo?" Harlan's girlfriend, Amber, said as they stood together in the crowded school hallway. "Earth to Harlan."

"What?" he said, eyes suddenly focused on her.

"You're not listening to me, that's what."

"Am so."

"Then what did I just say?"

"You were talking about how you went shopping. At the mall."

Amber glared back at him. "I don't know how you do it."

It's not that hard, Harlan thought. She was *always* talking about shopping at the mall. Either that or her role as Guinevere in the school production of *Camelot*.

"You are so slick," Amber went on. "You're a—what's the word? Rube?"

"Rake," Harlan said. "A rube is a hick. Or maybe you mean 'rogue'?"

"No, I'll go with 'rake.' That sounds right. Rhymes with 'snake.'"

Harlan met her grin for grin. Amber was blond and beautiful, but he was no mere planet orbiting blindly around her. No, he was the center of this solar system, not her.

"It's like what you said to Mrs. Woodburn in English today," Amber said. "How do you get away with stuff like that? That's sexual harassment, you know that?"

"No," Harlan said. "It's only sexual harassment if you're old and fat and bald. I'm seventeen and hunky, so it's just me being charming."

Amber rolled her eyes. "Where do you wanna go for lunch today?"

"What?" Harlan said, suddenly uneasy.

"Lunch?" Amber said. "Off-campus? What we do every single day at noon?"

But Harlan barely heard her. In his mind, he had been transported to a different place and time. The surroundings there were shadowy and indistinct, but one thing was very clear: in that place, Harlan was choking. In his mind's eye he struggled, gagging, trying to cough up whatever was in his throat. It wasn't working; he was suffocating, and no one was helping him. Harlan was experiencing all this, feeling the fear and anxiety of choking, even the bodily sensations—a sharp, throbbing ache in his throat. But at the same time, he was outside the vision, watching it all from one side, engulfed by the images, as if in an IMAX theater of the mind, but unable to affect the outcome.

The experience was also silent—completely, eerily silent. Was it a premonition of lunch that afternoon? That part still wasn't clear, but it sure felt like he was seeing the future.

"Harlan?" Amber said.

"What!" he said, jumping. Harlan was a lot of

things, but he'd never been jumpy, at least not until these past few weeks.

"Are you okay?"

"Yeah," Harlan said, his mouth dry as toast. "I'm fine."

The vision had gone as quickly as it had come. But the effects lingered. Harlan was flushed, his pulse pounding.

The fact is, it wasn't just the characters in *The Scarlet Letter* who had two faces. Lately, Harlan did too. One face was calm, cool, and collected, always steady, always in control—one of the load-bearing social supports that kept Roosevelt High School from collapsing. That face had been elected student body president by the largest margin in school history.

But the other face of Harlan Chesterton? Not so confident—in fact, downright fearful. And moody. And easily distracted.

There was a reason, of course. For the past few weeks, Harlan had been having these occasional premonitions of disaster—visions of what seemed to be the future, usually of death. At least they'd started out as occasional. Now he was having them two or more times a day.

Were they really foretelling the future? Harlan

had never had the nerve to find out. Once he had "foreseen" something, he did everything he could to avoid the time and place in which it seemed likely to occur.

"Are you sure you're okay?" Amber asked.

"What do you mean?" Harlan said, determined to keep from shaking.

"You look funny."

"I'm *fine*."

"Okay, okay." Amber sighed. "So what do you say?"

"About what?"

"About what I was saying!"

But this time, when Harlan tried to guess what Amber was referring to, nothing came up. What was it that she had been talking about? Suddenly he couldn't remember.

"Lunch!" Amber said. "Where do you want to go?"

Right then, an image of himself choking once again torpedoed through his mind. It was just as all-consuming, just as silent. And once again Harlan was forced to watch, and to feel the experience, but was unable to control or affect the outcome.

"Harlan?" Amber said.

"What!" he said, jumping again. "I'm skipping

lunch today!" he said, almost a shout. "I have to study."

"Are you serious?"

"I've got to go talk to someone," Harlan said. "I'll see you later, okay?"

And without waiting for an answer, he turned and walked away. It felt more like running, though, and in a way, that was exactly what it was.

If there really were two Harlan Chestertons these days, there was still one place where they came together—the swimming pool after school during his swim team workout. And why not? Mind and body joined together while he was swimming; it seemed only right that the two Harlans should come together there too.

Harlan lived to swim. He thought of it as flying— defying gravity, breaking the bonds of earthbound existence.

He'd heard people complain before about the heaviness of water, about how it could swallow you up or about its darkness. But for Harlan, water was liquid light, and swimming was freedom itself.

He hadn't always felt this way. He remembered the first time he'd been to a pool, when he was three years old and his mom had taken him to the golf club for his first swimming lesson. Harlan had had a fit, had refused to even put his foot into the water. But his mom hadn't pressured him like most of the other moms. No, she had simply brought him back to the pool, day after day, sitting with him by the pool's edge while the other kids had their lessons. Halfway through the summer, Harlan finally decided to join them in the water. He'd loved it, of course. And by the time he was seven, he was ready for the swim team.

So he had his mother to thank for his love of swimming? That was ironic, Harlan thought, especially given his feelings for her lately.

He was halfway through the warm-up before his buddy Ricky showed up. They'd been working out together since they were nine. Ricky knew him better than anyone else in the world.

"'S'up?" Ricky asked, long and lean in his black Speedo. Ricky Loduca was Guamanian—his birth parents had been born in Guam—which basically gave him as much street cred as being black, but without all the racism.

"Hey!" Harlan said, grinning.

"Let's do it," Ricky said, hopping into the pool alongside Harlan. But right before they pushed off, Ricky asked, "Hey, you drive to school today?"

"Yeah," Harlan said.

"Cool," Ricky said. "I have to leave early." On days that Harlan rode to school with Amber, Ricky usually drove him home.

"It's cool," Harlan said.

And then they were swimming side by side, in a lane all their own. As he finished his warm-up, Harlan immediately felt a connection with Ricky. People sometimes asked him if it got lonely, spending all that time underwater, alone with your thoughts. But for Harlan, swimming was the opposite of lonely. No, swimming was all about connection. It was about being totally attuned to the swimmers around you, feeling their wakes, drawing on their energy. When Harlan swam a set side by side with Ricky, they supported one another, pushing each other to swim faster, pulling each other when one fell behind. He may have been "alone" underwater, but he wasn't really.

Hey, you drive to school today? Suddenly, Ricky's totally innocuous question replayed in Harlan's brain. What did it have to do with anything? But because Harlan was thinking about driving, not focused on swimming, the connection with Ricky suddenly broke. He was still swimming side by side with him, but now Harlan was alone.

And inside his head, he was suddenly in a different place and time. A city street at night? A truck—or was it a van?—was bearing down on Harlan. He could see the expanding headlights, could watch the vehicle veering to one side as the driver tried to swerve away at the last second.

It was too late. The van still caught Harlan head-on. (Was Harlan in a car too? That part wasn't clear.) Everything that followed seemed to happen simultaneously: the fan of flashing sparks, the shattering glass, the wrenching metal, and—overwhelming everything else—the searing, straight-to-the-core-of-his-being pain. And it was all happening in perfect silence.

Harlan was having another premonition. But in the swimming pool? That was the one place where he felt most at home in the whole world.

Not today. The same vision swept back through his mind, like the backwash from a crashing wave. The van tried to swerve, then smashed into him once again. Harlan's heart pounded—wild, exploding pulsings that replaced the quick, even beats from the workout itself. This car crash was going to happen—Harlan *knew* it!

Harlan was coughing. Like he'd swallowed water. He wasn't swimming forward anymore. Now he was paddling upright in the water, but gasping for air.

A wave splashed in his face, causing him to swallow more water. Harlan began to struggle—flailing, almost.

Like he was drowning.

Which was impossible. Harlan could never drown—he *loved* the water! So why was he struggling now?

In an instant, Ricky was at his side, treading water, holding him up. The connection was back—in a way. Now they weren't supporting each other; now it was just Ricky supporting him.

"Har? You okay?" The concern in Ricky's eyes was obvious, even through swim goggles.

Harlan coughed. "I'm fine," he said. "I just swallowed some water."

Ricky stared at him. He knew that swimmers like the two of them never "swallowed water," at least not the way Harlan had. It would be like a star baseball pitcher suddenly falling off the mound. It just didn't happen.

Harlan pushed away, treaded water on his own. He hesitated, waiting for the premonition to come crashing back yet again. But it didn't.

"It's okay," Harlan said at last. "I'm fine. Let's just keep going, okay?"

Ricky finally nodded and they pushed off, swimming side by side again. But for Harlan, the memory of his latest premonition trailed behind him like an anchor.

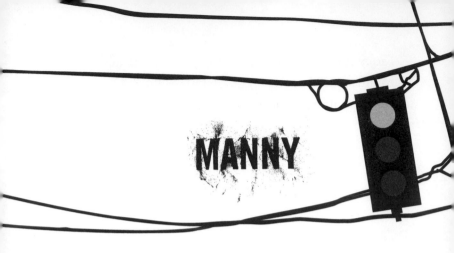

MANNY

EVERYTHING WAS OUT OF FOCUS. Manny had to squint to see what was going on in the theater in front of him. Problem was, he wasn't in a movie theater. He was in a stage theater—or "thea-*tuh*", as the actors liked to quip—with rehearsals of the school play taking place before him. So the problem wasn't an out-of-focus movie projector. No, the problem was him— a pounding headache that was affecting his eyesight. He squeezed his temples and that helped with his headache, but it didn't put anything back into focus.

"You okay?" said Keith, his assistant in the lighting booth.

"Huh?" Manny said. "Oh, yeah. Just tired." He was quick to change the subject. "We're still going to need those forest gobos for the fairy scenes. Did you ever track them down?"

"Backstage, I think."

Manny stared at Keith, oily-faced and gangly, too tall for his folding chair.

"Maybe I should go get 'em, huh?" Keith said.

"Thanks," Manny said, and in a second he was thankfully, blissfully, alone again. He looked down at the control panel in front of him. He loved the thought that from this seat he could control every single one of the sixty-two lights suspended from the ceiling of the theater in front of him—each lantern painstakingly plotted, gelled (or not), hung, and focused by Manny, and Manny alone. As a result, he controlled the look and feel of everything that happened down on that stage. Did that make him a control freak? Maybe not, but it definitely made him a geek. Let's face it, to the rest of the school, lighting design was just a notch above Chess Club—and even that was probably an overly optimistic assessment.

Okay, so Manny Tucker was a geek. He knew it, and he was okay with it. No, really. It didn't bother him. Not at all. Yes, he did lighting design, but he was damn good at it—a Barbizon Award regional finalist two years running (with an excellent shot at being named national winner this year!). What was the deal with being popular, anyway? Why would anyone want to have to spend two hundred dollars for the "right" pair of pants? It was just so much easier to wear black all the time like the other backstage geeks.

He looked up at the stage where Amber Hodges—Guinevere in the school's production of *Camelot*—was running through the dance steps to the "Lusty Month of May" number. She was the perfect example of how crazy it was to be popular. Why would anyone want to be in the spotlight like that? Why would she want the pressure of all those eyes on her? Though, Manny had to admit, she was kind of hot.

Okay, more than kind of hot. Gorgeous. She almost sparkled, and it had nothing whatsoever to do with Selma's costumes or Manny's lighting. The rest of the stage might be out of focus, but Amber couldn't ever be.

"Hey, Moonbeam," said a voice from behind. "Better get a Kleenex for that drool."

"Huh?" Manny jumped; he'd always been jumpy, and he hated himself for it. Jerry Blain was suddenly alongside him in the lighting booth. Amber's boyfriend? No, she hung with a different jock—same model, slightly different exterior. But what was Jerry Blain doing in the school theater—much less in Manny's lighting booth?

"Sorry?" Manny said to him.

Jerry laughed. "I see you starin'! Too bad you don't got a pair of X-ray specs, huh?"

"I'm the lighting designer. It's my job to stare at Amber Hodges."

"Not like that, it isn't!"

"What's it to you, anyway?" Manny said.

"Just don't get any ideas, Moonbeam. She's *way* out of your league."

Wait a minute, Manny thought. The lighting booth was *his* territory! Jerry wasn't even supposed to be *in* here! So why didn't Manny say something?

Because he was a geek, that's why. And while that meant he didn't have to worry about spending two hundred dollars on a pair of pants, the result was he had no power whatsoever. It also meant he wasn't allowed to talk to—or, apparently, even *look* at— Amber Hodges.

"What do you want, anyway?" Manny asked him.

"Just out in the hallway waiting for my buds," Jerry said. "Thought I'd come and see what's happening back in loserville."

"Well, I'm busy, okay?"

"O-kay!" Jerry said, enunciating like a kindergarten teacher. "But keep your eyes on the control board, Moonbeam, otherwise you'll need a Kleenex for more than just drool."

And with that he turned to go, laughing as he went.

Manny still had a headache, and the caffeine in his double shot of espresso was only making things worse. He'd come to this coffee shop to talk with his friend Elsa about the video they were making together. The movie was called *Momster*, and it was about how terrifying a mother could look from the point of view of a small child. But right now their video was the last thing on his mind.

Elsa had a face like the moon—soft and pleasing, with an actual glow (and an admittedly pockmarked surface). She was also deaf, which meant that she used ASL—American Sign Language.

It's all about perspective, she said, motioning with her hands. *We need to force the perspective to make the mother look really, really scary.*

That shouldn't be too hard. Manny answered in ASL too. His signing was more than decent, which made sense given all the time they'd spent together.

Part of me wishes we could cast a real child, Elsa went on. *But it'd be such a hassle to work with him. Besides, I guess it's funnier if we just dress an older actor in baby clothes.*

Manny nodded. An adult actor playing the child. It was a good idea—like most of Elsa's ideas. She had this great sense of the visual, of pattern and design. Was it because she was deaf, or was that a stereotype? All Manny knew was that he loved doing creative projects with her. It had been strange when they'd first met back in the fourth grade, her deafness. But it was immediately clear that they were kindred spirits; he'd never met anyone else so into the arts. So they hadn't let the language barrier come in the way of their becoming best friends. (It helped that Manny hadn't *had* any other friends!) Soon they'd collaborated on a whole string of creative projects: movies, websites, even an annual haunted house in her garage. Manny had never felt more alive than on the warm summer nights he spent over at Elsa's house, planning their latest project. Or waking up on a Saturday morning, knowing he had a full day to spend with his friend—and at least two days before he had to drag himself back to the dreariness of school again.

Which was why it was so frustrating that he hadn't been able to concentrate on any of their projects lately. He couldn't go on like this. Somehow he needed to get back in control. And maybe he could start by laying off the double shots of espresso and finding some aspirin for his headache.

Out of the corner of his eye, Manny saw Elsa making waving motions at him. He looked up at her.

What's wrong? she signed.

So she'd noticed he'd zoned out on her. It's rude to look away from anyone while she's talking, but it was doubly rude to do it to Elsa; looking away from a deaf person who signed made it impossible for her *to* talk.

Nothing, Manny signed. *Just tired. I'm sorry.*

Another nightmare?

He wished he'd never told Elsa about the nightmares. He'd been having them for weeks now. It hadn't been every night at first, but it was now. It was bad enough that he had to dream them; he didn't want to also have to *talk* about them.

Manny nodded glumly.

The same thing happen? Elsa signed.

He stood up from his chair. *Do you want a biscotti? I want a biscotti.*

You hate biscotti, Elsa said. *Everyone hates biscotti. Don't change the subject.*

He sank back down into his chair. *The dreams are nothing. It's no big deal.*

Elsa just stared at him. She didn't need to make motions with her hands for him to know what she was thinking; it was all written right there on her face. *If they're nothing,* she signed at last, *why do you keep having them?*

They'll go away, he said.

Eventually. But what are you going to do in the meantime?

Elsa was right. It wasn't just his eyes that were out of focus; it was his whole life. And he just knew that he would keep having these nightmares until he somehow got his life back into focus. The nightmares were *about* the fact that his life was out of focus. But how did a person go about putting his *life* back into focus?

We can make an oversized papier-mâché baby rattle! Manny suddenly signed, changing the subject again. *So it'll make our actor look like a real baby. And maybe a great big rocking chair?*

This time, Elsa took the bait. Her face broke into a smile and she was off and running, building on his idea with another one of her own.

It was after eleven o'clock, and Manny was exhausted.

Exhausted, yes, but also frightened—by his bed, of all things. Who ever heard of a person being afraid of his *bed*?

It looked perfectly comfortable—*was* perfectly

comfortable. His dad was embarrassed that he wasn't able to afford new sheets for Manny to replace his *Lord of the Rings* ones from a few years back. But Manny loved those sheets, even at age seventeen. And there was a thick layer of blankets, just the way he liked it. He loved the cozy feel of all that material pressing down against his body.

Of course, Manny's fear wasn't really about the bed itself; it was about his dreams. He couldn't bear the thought of another nightmare.

He looked over at his computer. As much as the bed repelled him, the computer seemed to be enticing him, calling to him, drawing him close. He'd already updated his blog for the day—twice—but he couldn't go to bed without checking his e-mail one more time.

He did, and found nothing. Not even any spam.

As long as he was online, he decided to surf over to a couple of his "favorites." But there weren't any new postings on any of his online friends' blogs, and there wasn't anything going on in any of his usual chat rooms.

He glanced at the backpack lying next to his desk.

Homework! He still had homework to do!

Okay, so maybe he didn't have any homework *per se*. But he could always review his notes.

Review his notes? Manny had never "reviewed his notes" in his entire life. What was he thinking?

He looked back at the computer screen, but now it was blurry too. He rubbed his eyes, but that just made his headache worse.

Manny needed to go to sleep.

He turned to the bed again. The way the blankets were askew, it looked like the bed was grinning at him. Ironically, he couldn't even count on lying awake, tossing and turning. He knew he'd fall asleep just moments after his head hit the pillow. It wasn't until he woke up in the middle of the night, pulse pounding and sheets drenched in sweat, that he wouldn't be able to get back to sleep again.

He sighed. There was no point in trying to delay the inevitable. He stood up, stripped down to his Jockey shorts, and climbed into bed. With that, he braced himself for the worst, and closed his eyes.

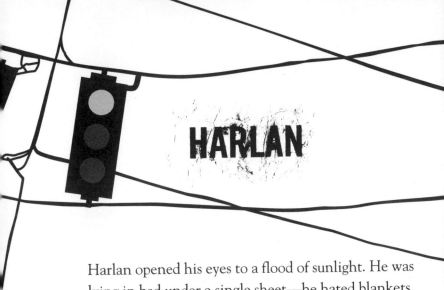

HARLAN

Harlan opened his eyes to a flood of sunlight. He was lying in bed under a single sheet—he hated blankets, even in winter, so at some point during the night he'd kicked the bedspread off. But he'd fallen asleep with his curtains open, and now the clear morning light filled his room like a liquid, cleansing and clarifying every surface.

It was Saturday, he realized. No school.

He looked around. He couldn't get over how different everything looked, how the world almost glowed. It was like he'd woken up in a commercial for laundry detergent.

He started laughing.

He couldn't help it. It wasn't just the darkness that the daylight had washed away; it was everything—the gloom, the anxiety, the fear. This morning, he actually felt giddy. He couldn't remember feeling this good in weeks. Oh, he remembered feeling lousy in the days before, and he remembered why: his premonitions of disaster. His last premonition had been the one in the swimming pool, where he'd imagined he would be hit by a van. That had been one situation he could definitely not avoid; after all, it's not like he could never get into a car again. And so, after the workout, he had—slowly and cautiously—driven home.

Nothing had happened. He hadn't even *seen* a van, much less come close to being hit by one.

And in the light of this brand-new day, the whole incident just seemed so utterly ridiculous. No one could predict the future. He saw that now. How could he have been so stupid?

There was an urgent knock on the door. "Harlan? What's wrong?" His mom.

"Nothing," he said.

The door swung open. "What was that I heard?"

"Me," Harlan said. "I was laughing."

"Oh." She stared at him. "Why?" His mom thought something was wrong because he'd burst into spontaneous laughter. Somehow, every problem with their relationship could be found right there in that one little exchange.

"Because I felt like it," Harlan said. "Because I felt good."

She kept staring at him. The first thing people always said about his mother was that she was beautiful. Harlan supposed that was true. She certainly had the "look"—the hair, the clothes, the makeup (*especially* the makeup; it had been so long since he'd seen her without it that he honestly couldn't remember what she looked like). She definitely didn't appear to be an ordinary mom; she didn't *feel* like an ordinary mom either. To Harlan, she was more like the *idea* of a mom than a real person. The words and actions had all been there—the unqualified praise for his sixth-grade dried-leaf collection, the obligatory attendance at the most important of his swim meets. But they felt hollow somehow, a little too deliberate, too perfect—like the motions of the animatronic robots inside a ride at Disney World. Especially lately.

"You should get moving," she said.

Moving? he thought. But even as he thought this, he remembered. He had a morning swim workout, then SAT Prep at the community college, a practice session of French Debate, and finally his volunteer work with deaf kids at the YMCA.

Suddenly he didn't feel so giddy anymore.

"Oh, and your father's invited you to a banquet tonight," his mom went on. "The Bittle Society."

His father: United States Senator Lawrence M. Chesterton, Very Big Cheese. Was it his imagination, or did the morning sunlight just dim? As for the Bittle Society, that was a local organization that—well, Harlan wasn't exactly sure *what* they did. As far as he could tell, it was a group of filthy-rich people who sat around congratulating themselves for being so rich—and for being smart enough to elect a politician like his dad, who did everything in his power to keep them rich.

"But Ricky and Amber and I are going to a party tonight," Harlan began, "and I said—"

"A party?" his mom interrupted. "Will there be drinking?"

Harlan rolled his eyes. "Mom." She was always going on about her fear of his drinking or taking drugs—mostly, he was sure, because of how it would make his dad look if it ever got out to the press.

"Well, it doesn't matter," his mother said, "because your father's getting an award tonight, and you need to be there. Besides, this is one of the few weekends he gets to spend at home. He wants to spend it with you. Don't you want to spend it with him?"

This was typical of his mom—a precise combination of obligation and guilt. It was all spin, of course. His father got some kind of award every weekend he was home—usually from organizations like the Bittle Society. And if the Senator had really wanted to spend time with Harlan, he would have taken him to a baseball game. No, what he and Harlan's mom really wanted was to use their son in the latest of an endless series of photo ops. He wasn't sure why he had even bothered raising an objection. Harlan had learned long ago that there were some battles you just couldn't win.

He started to slide out of bed, but stopped. "Do you mind?" If his mom wasn't going to let him see her without makeup, he wasn't going to let her see him in his boxers.

Harlan stared at the wall—why would anyone put carpeting on a wall?—and wondered how many banquets like this one he'd gone to in his life. Five hundred? A thousand? He had to have been to at least fifty in this very hall. He thought, Maybe I should start scratching hatch marks in one of the bathroom stalls.

Since the evening had started, Harlan's father had spoken to him a grand total of three sentences, and they had all been in the car on the ride over. So much for his father's wanting to spend time with him.

"You look like you want to be here even less than I do," said a voice from one side. For cocktails, everyone was still standing.

"What?" Harlan said. It was a woman—in her mid-thirties, nice-looking but not beautiful. Somehow Harlan knew in a glance that a Bittle Society dinner was not her natural habitat. Her outfit, for example. White blouse, purple skirt, silver jewelry—not inexpensive, but nothing remotely high-fashion, everything chosen to last. In fact, now that Harlan looked at her, he could swear the woman looked familiar. "No," he told her, maybe a little too firmly. "Not at all."

The woman smiled. "Relax. It's not that obvious."

"I know you," Harlan said suddenly. "You're Beth Farrell. The novelist." Always address people by their names, Harlan's mother said. Studies show that the sound people most like to hear is their own name spoken out loud.

"That's me," said the woman. "Ever read any of my books?"

"I—" He hadn't, but he wondered if he should lie. He knew his mother would want him to. On the other hand, it seemed like such an obvious lie, so easy to expose. "No," he said at last. "But now I will."

"Don't bother. I just like asking people that. I can always tell when they're lying. And you'd be shocked how often that is."

Now Harlan smiled. He liked her.

"I'm Harlan—"

"Chesterton," she finished. "The senator's son. I know who you are." Harlan wasn't surprised. Everyone always knew who he was.

"So, Ms. Farrell—"

"Beth."

"You're a member of the Bittle Society?"

"Um, no." She leaned closer and lowered her voice. "Bunch of right-wing bluenoses, but don't quote me on that." Her hair smelled like a forest of cedar and pine, as if she'd been out hiking in the woods that very afternoon. "Still," Beth went on, "just because they're Republican, that doesn't mean I won't take their money. I'm here to get an award, just like your dad."

As if by reflex, they both turned to look at Harlan's father, holding court over by the hors d'oeuvres—close, but not too close, to the bar. His dad adjusted his glasses. He looked mild-mannered because he was; Harlan's mom was the power behind that throne.

"Must be tough," Beth said.

"What?" Harlan said.

"Having a father like that."

He knew he should be nervous, talking to someone unfamiliar about something as personal as this—especially given that she was a writer. He knew what his mother would say about a situation like this: smile politely and change the subject.

"It's not that bad," Harlan said.

"Uh-huh." She obviously didn't believe him. "So are you planning on following him into politics?"

"Probably," Harlan said. In some families, it went without saying that the children would go to college. In his family, it went without saying that Harlan would go into politics (*and* go to college!). He'd been groomed for it his whole life. And he already knew he would be very good at it.

"So is that what you really want to do?" Beth asked.

"What?" Harlan said. He'd been asked a lot of questions at functions like this, but he'd never been asked that one before.

But suddenly there was his mom, appearing out of thin air. "Beth!" she said, all popcorn and pinwheels on the surface, but Harlan could hear the creaking of very thin ice under her breath.

"Victoria," Beth said to his mother. The feeling was obviously mutual.

"Excuse us, please," his mother said to the novelist. "There's someone I want Harlan to meet."

Harlan knew there wasn't really anyone his mom wanted him to meet. She just didn't want him talking to Beth Farrell.

"It was very nice to meet you, Harlan," Beth said, but his mother was already ushering him away, like a Secret Service agent whisking the president away from a would-be assassin.

"So," Harlan said to his mother when they were away from Beth and the crowd. "It's been an hour, and I talked to twenty-five people. Twenty-six, if you count Beth Farrell. I'm leaving, okay?"

"Leaving?" His mother was predictably horrified. "We haven't even had dinner! And what about the award?"

"I told you this morning: Ricky and Amber and I are going to a party. I can call him, and he'll come pick me up."

But as they talked, Harlan sensed that Bruce, his father's chief of staff, had pricked up his ears, even several clusters of people away. His mom noticed too.

In a second, Bruce was at their side, all pomaded and twitchy. "You're leaving?" he said to Harlan.

Harlan nodded hesitantly.

"What?" his mom said to Bruce.

"It's just that you know how the senator's numbers are down among Asian-Americans," Bruce said.

Harlan just listened. The scary part was, he already knew exactly where this was headed.

"What are you saying?" his mom asked Bruce.

"I'm saying that a family visit to that Thousand Cranes League banquet later tonight might make one hell of a Christmas card."

Bruce and Harlan's mother both turned to look, full-bore, at Harlan.

"Mom—" he started to say.

"Not here, Harlan," she said. That was the rule: absolutely no dissension in public. But apparently it only counted as dissension when he disagreed with his mother, not when she disagreed with him.

Bruce smiled at him; whenever he smiled, he reminded Harlan of a child molester. "Just an hour, Sport. That okay?"

Harlan shrugged. "I guess." Then he turned to go.

"Where are you going?" his mom asked.

"Outside for a smoke."

"Harlan! Not where people can see!"

"Smoking?" Bruce said to Harlan's mom, concerned. "Since when did he start smoking?"

"It's a joke," Harlan said. "I don't really smoke."

"Thank God," Bruce said. Then he added, with another pathetic smile, "That stuff'll kill you, Sport."

"Harlan, you know better than to make jokes like that," his mother said, already turning away. "Someone might overhear."

The fog was thick in the streets outside the convention center. If it hadn't been for the sidewalks, he'd probably have been wandering in circles.

Harlan wasn't an idiot. He knew what Beth Farrell had been insinuating back in the convention hall. *So is that what you really want to do?* She'd been saying he was just doing what his parents wanted him to do. Well, no duh! Harlan knew he didn't have control over his life. He never had. Oh, sure, he had control at school—almost complete control, even over the teachers, which was kind of ironic when you thought about it. But that was all small stuff. The big stuff, the story line of his life, he was powerless to change. It was a little like the premonitions themselves, really: he could watch his life, like on a viewscreen, but he couldn't direct it.

It was so much easier this way. Beth Farrell had no idea of the kinds of forces his parents could bring to bear on a person in order to get their way. His mom ran their family life like she ran his dad's reelection campaign—namely, to win. That meant she had no problem playing hardball when she had to. Once, when he was in the seventh grade, Harlan had been acting slightly rebellious at home. Then his Boy Scout troop, which had been about to hold its annual fund-raiser, found that the restaurant that was donating the food suddenly had "problems" with the Health Department inspectors. Word quickly leaked that it was all Harlan's fault; everyone—from the other scouts, to the troop leaders, to the owners of the restaurant—had been furious with him. Needless to say, Harlan had quickly fallen back in line with his parents, just as he had done so many times since then.

The fog surrounded Harlan now, so thick he could barely make anything out. It was like being in an alien world, some planet without substance, a place of steam and gas. Or maybe it was a passageway between worlds, a shifting corridor through the swirling mists of time. The fog smelled musty, like frayed furniture in a long-abandoned house.

Is that what you really want to do? That's what Beth Farrell had asked. But Harlan wasn't sure *what* he wanted to do with his life. He was seventeen years old—how *could* he know? And until he figured that out, he might as well do what his parents said.

Someday, he'd figure out what *he* wanted. Then he'd stand up to his parents.

Someday. Just not now. Now he had to get back to the convention hall before his mom called out the FBI.

But which was the way back? He turned himself around, looking for a sign or landmark. Suddenly Harlan realized he was lost in the fog. It flowed around him like paint being swirled in a can, pressing in on him, confusing him. It made him dizzy. The fog even seemed to muffle sound.

But he wasn't lost, not really. He took a deep breath of the stale air, trying to clear his head. He knew this city. Besides, he couldn't have walked more than six or seven blocks. He just needed to keep walking until he came to a building or landmark that he recognized.

A pair of street signs materialized out of the fog. He had reached an intersection. The corner of Grand and Humble.

Everything was okay. Harlan knew this intersection. He hadn't gone more than three blocks from the convention center. Maybe he'd been walking around in circles after all.

He stepped off the curb, into the crosswalk.

And right into the path of an oncoming bus.

MANNY

Manny braced himself for the blow, but it didn't come.

He looked around. He was standing on a wide, sandy beach in the middle of a scorcher of a day. But *was* it a beach? When he looked for the ocean, he didn't see it. The sand sloped downward like a beach, and he definitely smelled the ocean, but there didn't seem to be any water. How had he come to be in this place anyway? It was like he had just appeared here, as if in a dream.

And why was he bracing himself? Why had he been so certain there was a blow coming?

There were people near him, a man and woman in their late twenties. They definitely weren't dressed for the beach. He was wearing a tuxedo, and she was wearing an elegant black dress. They were hurrying away from Manny, up the sand, and he couldn't see their faces. But they looked familiar somehow.

"Manny?" a voice said from behind.

It was his dad. He was dressed as a lifeguard—in red shorts and a white T-shirt that read "Lifeguard," even with a whistle around his neck.

"Dad?" Manny said. "Why are you dressed like that?" His dad wasn't a lifeguard; he worked as a paralegal.

"It doesn't matter," his dad said. "Come on, let's eat." He gestured toward a table in the sand. It had been set with a crisp white tablecloth, crystal goblets, and silver serving dishes. It looked nothing like a table his dad would set. It looked like a table that the man in the tuxedo and the woman in the dress would eat at. Why had his dad taken their table?

"This doesn't look right," Manny said. "I don't think we should be here."

"Why not?" his dad said, smiling. "Sit. Eat." He guided Manny toward the table and set him down—firmly—into one of the two chairs. "Now eat."

"But, Dad—"

The plate in front of Manny was covered with a lustrous silver lid. His dad lifted it. But it wasn't food on the plate underneath; it was a pair of broken wire-rim glasses. The frames were bent and twisted, the lenses shattered.

"Dad?" Manny said, confused. "What *is* this?"

"What?" his dad said innocently. "Eat." He poured something from a decanter into Manny's crystal goblet; it looked and smelled like gasoline. "And drink."

"But I can't eat or drink that!" Manny said.

His dad didn't answer. He wasn't listening. He was staring over at the area where the ocean should have been, a blank expression on his face.

"Dad?" Manny said. "What is it?"

His dad turned to him and smiled again, but this time it was an unfamiliar grin—dark, unsettling. The instant Manny registered that smile, a shadow fell over them both, like something had blotted out the sun. Manny felt a rumble, heard a roar that grew louder by the second.

He glanced up. It wasn't just the sun that had been blotted out. It was the entire sky.

Blotted out the sky? What could blot out the *sky*?

Then he knew. *"Tidal wave!"* he shouted. That's why there hadn't been any ocean—it had all been sucked out into the massive wave! "We need to get out of here! We need to *run*!"

He glanced up at his dad again, but now his father's face was all in shadows. Even so, and even over the roar of the wave, Manny could tell that his dad was laughing.

And then the wave crashed down on top of them.

At the instant of impact, Manny woke up. He sat up in bed. He was soaking wet, but not from any wave. From sweat.

Manny shuffled into the kitchen feeling like the Mummy—the shambling, lethargic mummy from the original movies in the 1930s, not the agile, computer-animated one from the crappy remakes.

"Well," his dad said, seated at the table, looking up from his newspaper. "You look like hell."

"Uh-huh," Manny said, pouring a cup of tea from a pot on the counter. It had been a good four hours since he'd woken up from the nightmare—of course he hadn't been able to get back to sleep—but it still felt weird to be with his dad. The strangest thing about the dream was how out of character his dad had acted. Now it felt like one of those movie scenes when the character thinks he's awake, but is really still in the nightmare. Manny almost expected his dad to leap up from the table brandishing the knife from *Psycho*.

"Another nightmare, huh?" his dad said.

Manny nodded, searching for a clean plate.

"And to think you could be dreaming about sex like most teenage boys."

"Dad," Manny said. "Do you mind?"

"What? You don't wanna talk about sex with your dad? Why in the world not?"

"Dad!" But Manny couldn't keep from smiling. The truth was, his dad was the opposite of nightmarish. He was best described as boyish—clean-shaven and bouncy, often impetuous, more like an older brother than a dad. Of course, that didn't mean he couldn't also be strict, like the time he wouldn't let Manny and Elsa go to that *Xena: Warrior Princess* convention in Pasadena, California. But at least he always let Manny make his case. Manny's dad was pretty much the perfect authority figure—someone who had actually earned, and *deserved*, respect.

"I had a dream too," his dad was saying. "I was the Head Munchkin, and I had to deny membership in the Lollipop Guild to the Keebler Elves."

Okay, so maybe the Munchkin dream didn't make Manny's dad sound like some awesome authority figure. But the fact that he was willing to say things like that was exactly what made Manny's dad so great. He also loved to cook, kept houseplants, even hugged his son. Manny had always wondered what it meant that he had such an emotionally accessible dad; was that what had made him one of the arty-fruity types at school? He also wondered how his dad had ended up such a nontraditional guy. Was it because he'd had to be both father and mother to Manny? Manny's mom had died when Manny was two months old. Skin cancer, his dad had said once. It was one of the things Manny and his dad didn't talk about—one of the very few things.

"So," his dad said, suddenly all ears. "Tell me about *your* dream."

Manny glanced at the clock on the stove. "Shouldn't you be on your way to work?"

His dad sipped his tea. "I can be a little late. Come on. *Talk.*"

Manny dished up two fried eggs from the pan on the stove. "I got creamed by a tidal wave."

"I think I'm detecting a pattern. What was it last night? A herd of elephants? And before that, it was a locomotive. Didn't you actually get hit by a falling safe once? Or maybe it was an anvil."

"There was one thing different," Manny said.

"Really? Do tell."

"You were in it."

"Me? What'd I do?"

Manny considered lying, but he didn't seem to be able to do that to his dad. "Well, it's not real flattering."

"For you or for me?"

"Never mind."

"Me, huh? Hmmmm. Well, what'd I do?"

Manny took a seat at the table across from him. "You laughed at me."

Manny's dad just listened.

So Manny told him the dream—the well-dressed couple hurrying away; the plate of broken eyeglasses; the way his dad, dressed as a lifeguard, had laughed when the wave was crashing down on top of them. Maybe his dad could tell him what all this meant; he had a pretty good instinct about these things.

"So?" Manny said when he was done. "What do you think?"

His dad didn't answer right away. He was staring out the window. It was hard to tell what he was thinking. He wasn't even drinking his tea. Manny couldn't help but be reminded of the part of the nightmare when his dad had stopped and stared blankly out at the approaching tidal wave. At first he thought his dad was now trying to be funny—except then Manny remembered that he hadn't told his dad that part of the dream.

"Dad?"

Suddenly his dad stood up from the table. "Oh, God, I just remembered! I gotta drop off some dry cleaning." Was it Manny's imagination, or was his dad flustered? But he didn't get *flustered*—not by beautiful women, not by patronizing car mechanics, not by anything.

"Dad?" Manny said. "Are you okay? I didn't offend you or anything, did I?"

"Huh? You mean about the dream? Please."

"But—"

"Manny, I really gotta go. 'Bye!"

And then his dad was gone. Manny sat at the kitchen table, alone, the fried eggs on his plate looking up at him like a pair of broken spectacles.

Manny squatted down on his haunches, staring at the bushy gray cat ten feet or so ahead of him on the sidewalk. He stretched out his hand and twiddled his fingers. The trick, he knew, was to let the animal come to you. Cats didn't like their space invaded. Manny could relate.

He glanced at Elsa, who was waiting impatiently off to one side. *I can't believe you!* she signed. *We can't go anywhere without you stopping to pet the cats.*

I can't help it, Manny signed. *I like cats. I think it's rude to walk by and not say hi.*

No kidding!

He gave his fingers another wiggle, but the cat looked warily at Elsa. So that was the problem. The cat sensed Elsa was not a fan.

Just one more second, Manny said to Elsa. Making contact with this particular cat called for extreme measures. Slowly, he started inching forward.

The cat turned and loped into the bushes.

Manny gave up, and they started walking again. It was easier to talk to Elsa somewhere inside, face-to-face, so they could read each other's signs. But Manny couldn't bear being inside right now.

Elsa tapped him on the arm. He turned to look at her. *You had another nightmare, didn't you?* she signed.

How did you know? he asked.

I can just tell. Wanna talk about it?

Actually, he signed, *it's not the nightmare that's bugging me this time.*

Then what?

It's this morning, when I told my dad about the dream. At first, he said he wanted to hear it. But when I told him, he acted really weird.

Elsa frowned. *Weird how?*

I don't know, Manny said. *Nervous. Not like his usual self. Suddenly he couldn't get away from me fast enough.*

Maybe he's having a bad day.

Yeah. Well, no. I mean, he was his usual self until I told him about the nightmare. That's when he got weird.

Maybe you scared him, Elsa said. *Something in the dream.*

That's what I think too. Because he was in this one. He told Elsa about the nightmare.

Her eyes went wide. *That was your dream?*

Yeah. Why?

Is that the way you feel about your dad? That he doesn't listen to you? Or that he's supposed to be protecting you from something, but isn't?

No! Manny said. *Not at all! My dad's great. You know that.*

That's not the way the dream makes it sound.

Well, yeah. But it's just a dream.

Even so, Elsa said. *Maybe you offended him.*

Manny considered this. *Nah. My dad's not like that. Besides, he knows how I feel about him.* He thought back on their interaction in the kitchen. *The worst part was, when I told him about the dream, it was like a little bit of it came true. He turned into this person I didn't know at all. He stared out the window with this blank expression on his face, just like in the dream.*

Maybe he feels guilty, Elsa signed.

About what?

She exaggerated a shrug—one of the many ways she added emphasis to her hand gestures. *Who knows with parents? But it sounds like your dream hit a nerve. So what's he done to you to feel guilty about? You two have any big arguments lately?*

What Elsa was saying made sense, given his dad's weird reaction. But his dad hadn't done anything to feel guilty about—lately or ever. Manny shook his head again. *I don't think so.*

Maybe it's something you don't know about, Elsa said. *Something he's hiding. You should talk to him.*

Manny smiled. *Oh, come on! You know my dad. He couldn't hide anything.* Or could he? Manny wondered.

Oh, no! Elsa said, spotting something ahead of them. *Here we go again!*

It was another cat—a sleek black one this time—sitting on the sidewalk right in front of them.

Go ahead, Elsa said, rolling her eyes. *Say hi!*

But now Manny wasn't in any mood to pet a cat. Still, he knew it was expected. So he bent down again and held out his fingers.

This time the cat didn't even consider investigating his hand. No, it took one look at Manny—and only Manny, not Elsa—and turned to run under the steps of a nearby house. Once there, it crouched in the shadows, glaring out at Manny with the wide eyes and arched back of outright fear.

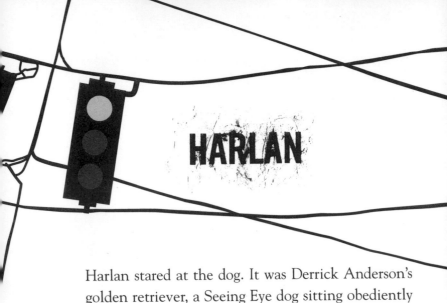

HARLAN

Harlan stared at the dog. It was Derrick Anderson's golden retriever, a Seeing Eye dog sitting obediently by his master's locker just down the hallway. Harlan loved dogs. He loved their strength and confidence, and their sense of loyalty to their owners. (That loyalty was probably why his mom had never let him have one; she didn't want anyone in the house who hadn't sworn fealty to her.)

But Harlan wasn't thinking about dogs just then. He was thinking about his near miss with that bus the previous Saturday night. It was just luck that he'd seen the bus and been able to pull himself back in time. If he hadn't, it would have slammed right into him, and he'd be dead for sure. It was easily the closest he'd ever come to dying.

And he'd seen it all in advance. He'd had that

premonition in the swimming pool, the one of the swerving "van," and it had come true. In other words, the strange mental pictures flashing through his brain weren't just random images—they really were actual glimpses into the future!

They also hadn't stopped. He was still experiencing the premonitions, each one a vision of his own death, each one different than before: Harlan trapped at the bottom of a slick-walled pit, Harlan plunging down a flight of massive stairs. None of these others had come true—yet!—but maybe that was only because he was back to avoiding any locations that were anything like ones he saw in his premonitions.

What was happening to him? Harlan couldn't figure it out. Even if the premonitions really were glimpses into the future, why had his life suddenly become so dangerous?

"Hey," Amber said, coming up to him in the hallway.

"Hey," Harlan said, his eyes still on Derrick's golden retriever. The premonition with the bus hadn't *exactly* come true; after all, he'd managed to avoid getting hit. And none of the other disasters had come true either—so far. Did that mean that he was merely seeing *possible* futures—that nothing was fixed and he could avoid them all if he tried hard enough?

"How are you?" Amber asked.

"Huh?" Harlan said. "Oh. Fine." Or maybe the bus in the fog had just been a coincidence. It's not like it was the first time he'd had a close call as a pedestrian. So maybe he was just suffering from some kind of hallucination. Not that that was a particularly comforting thought.

"Just for the record?" Amber said. "I'm fine too."

He tore his eyes away from Derrick's dog at last and turned to look at her. "Sorry. I'm a little preoccupied."

"No kidding. Been that way a lot lately. What's wrong?"

"What?"

"Something's wrong. What is it?"

He tried to laugh it off. "Nothing's wrong. What makes you think something's wrong?"

"Oh, I don't know. How about the fact that you just spent the last ten minutes staring off into space?"

Harlan blushed. Had anyone else noticed? He glanced around. People were looking over at him, but that didn't mean anything. He was Harlan Chesterton; people were always staring at him.

"It's nothing," Harlan said to Amber. "Just thinking about Woodburn's lecture."

"The Scarlet Letter?"

"Huh? Oh. Yeah." In-flippin'-credible. He had taken an already pitiful lie and actually made it sound even worse. He wasn't just losing his edge; it was long gone.

"Harlan," Amber said, already sounding weary. "I'm supposed to be your girlfriend. If you can't tell me the truth, why are we even together?"

The truth? No way could he tell her the truth. That he "saw" future disasters? He hadn't believed it at first; why should she?

"Harlan?"

"What?"

She just stared at him. He had to say something. If he didn't, she was going to make some kind of scene, probably eventually break up with him. That wouldn't be the worst thing in the world, but Harlan knew he didn't have the mental energy to deal with it anytime soon.

"It's my parents," Harlan said. There. That was something that was bothering him. It was "the truth."

"What about 'em?"

Harlan released a heavy sigh. "They don't let me live my own life."

"Of course not. They're your parents. What else is new?"

She started to turn away, but Harlan stopped her. "No. It's more than that. She picks my shirts. Hell, she's already picked out the state congressional district where I'm supposed to run for my first office when I graduate from college."

"Parents suck. But hey, it's not like yours are making you sleep in a closet."

"Come on, Amber. You know what I'm talking about. I mean, would it be such a terrible thing if I didn't go into politics?"

"You, not going into politics?"

"Yeah."

"Hel-looo! Student Body President!"

"That's not politics. That's a popularity contest."

"Harlan, have you watched the news lately? What do you think politics is?"

"This isn't about politics. It's about the fact that I don't get any say."

"Okay," Amber said. "What if you did have a choice? What do you wanna do?"

Harlan thought for a second, then shook his head. "I don't know. I'm seventeen years old. Why do I have to know? Why do I have to know anything?"

"Harlan." There was a strange edge to Amber's

voice. "Stop it. You're weirding me out."

He stared at her. She was actually serious. This talk, questioning his life, was unsettling her. Amber had signed up to be the girlfriend of the Senator's Son, the Student Body President, the confident rake who never questioned anything. Now he was changing, and that upset her.

Could she really be that shallow? And how had he never noticed that before?

"Hey!" Amber said, suddenly as light as a soap bubble. "I have an idea!"

"What?"

"Jerry Blain's having a party this weekend! His parents are going to Morocco."

"So?"

"So let's go! 'Kay?"

A party. That was the last place in the world Harlan wanted to be. It annoyed him that Amber couldn't see this. Or maybe she could see it and this was some kind of test: was he still the boyfriend she'd hooked up with, or was he already too far gone?

"Amber, I don't know."

"*Harlan.*" An actual whine. How had he also never noticed how much Amber whined?

"Okay, fine," he said. "We'll go to the damn party."

• • •

"*Dude!*" Ricky said, beer bottle in hand. "You *came!*"

It was Saturday night, at Jerry Blain's party, at Jerry's parents' house out on the lake. Make that *mansion* out on the lake. True, Harlan went to a public school, but only because it looked better to the voters. It was the newest, richest public high school in the city—his mom had made sure of that.

Anyway, a promise was a promise. Now here Harlan was, right by Amber's eager side. It was crowded, but not as mobbed as he'd expected. And the blaring music sounded slightly out of beat. Even the lights seemed unusually bright. Everything about this party was just a little off. Except, Harlan knew, it was really him that was off.

"Why'd you think I wouldn't come?" Harlan asked Ricky. Amber had already run off with her friends to giggle and do Jell-O shots.

"I dunno," Ricky said. "You just seem like you have a lot on your mind lately."

So Ricky knew something was up. Harlan wasn't surprised—Ricky had always been perceptive. Was it because he was gay? Ricky had come out the year before, in an article in the school newspaper. He'd even managed to stay popular, at least with girls. It helped that Ricky was a jock. And that he had never,

ever, not once, mentioned having a boyfriend, or that he found any particular guy good-looking, not even a singer or movie actor. Even in private to Harlan, supposedly his best friend.

"It's nothing," Harlan said. "Parent stuff. Hey, you ready for Wednesday's swim meet?" They were up against Harriet Tubman High School, one of their team's most notorious rivals.

But before Ricky could answer, Amber was back by Harlan's side, excited about something. "Hey, come here!" she said. "There's something I want you to see!"

Harlan looked at Ricky. "What's going on?"

Ricky shrugged. "Some game or somethin'."

Harlan let Amber lead him into the front room. A group of people had gathered around the glass coffee table, where someone had set up a Ouija board.

"Jeez," mumbled Ricky, who had followed behind. "Not a Ouija board."

Amber pulled him toward the table. "Come on, Harlan! Let's do it!"

It was a classic Harlan Chesterton moment. A couple of weeks earlier, Harlan knew he would have taken a seat at that board, asked a question, then spelled out some incredibly witty remark. It all would have come to him without thought, effortlessly. And it would have been so funny that people would still be talking about it the whole week following: *Can you* believe *what Harlan spelled out on that Ouija board!*

But now he felt strange, on the spot.

"What?" Harlan said. "No, Amber. Let someone else go. I wanna get a beer."

"Oh, come on! Don't be like that." She knew a Harlan Chesterton moment when she saw it too. All she wanted was a little of that old Harlan magic.

And now—thanks to Amber—everyone was calling for him, egging him on.

"Hey, Har," Ricky said casually. "Come here, you gotta see the hot tub in the backyard." So Ricky saw his discomfort and was trying to rescue him.

"He's busy!" Amber snapped at Ricky. "Come on, Harlan. Just try it."

In other words, even Ricky couldn't save him now.

Harlan approached the board. "I thought these things were supposed to be satanic," he said.

"Satanic? Us?" said Jerry Blain. "We'd never do anything *satanic*." He turned and called into the kitchen. "Hey, Beekman, bring me another bottle of babies' blood!"

Everyone laughed except Harlan. It was a funny

line, well delivered, but Harlan wasn't used to being the straight man for other people's jokes.

"Who's going with him?" Rachel Jones asked.

"Let me, let me!" Amber said. She practically leaped toward the board.

Harlan knelt down across the table from her. In the upper left corner of the Ouija board, there was a picture of the sun alongside the word "Yes"; in the upper right corner, there was a crescent moon with the word "No." In the middle of the board, two arced rows spelled out every letter in the alphabet, and underneath the letters was a straight row of numbers. On the board's surface, a big plastic pointer rested on three raised felt tips. Thanks to SAT Prep, Harlan knew that this was called a planchette, and that it supposedly spelled out mystical messages.

"Look," Ricky said, nodding to some writing on the bottom of the board. "The game's made by Milton Bradley. Oh, now that *is* scary!"

Everyone laughed; this time, Harlan laughed too. Good ol' Ricky.

He lifted his hands and rested his fingers lightly on his half of the plastic pointer.

And immediately knew he'd made a mistake. He could already feel it—a strange electricity in the air. Milton Bradley or not, this board could very well bring on another premonition. Or maybe it was all in his mind. Either way, Harlan wanted out.

"It's not moving," Harlan said, pulling his hands away. "Oh well!"

People chuckled. It wasn't really funny, but when people expect you to be a cutup, they pretty much laugh at anything you say. At least at first.

"Don't be stupid!" Amber said, and Harlan was keenly aware that she never would have spoken to him like that before, especially in public. "We have to ask it a question."

"So ask it a question," Harlan mumbled, resting his fingers back on the pointer. He wasn't going to have a premonition; he wouldn't let himself. There was too much at stake.

"Let's see," Amber said, thinking, putting her fingers on the pointer too. "I know! Will Harlan ever be elected president of the United States?"

He glared at her across the board. This was her way of goading him after what he'd said earlier in the week about not wanting to go into politics. Not only had he never noticed how much Amber whined, he had also never noticed just what a colossal bitch she was.

The plastic pointer jerked under his fingers.

"Ooooo!" said Brian Meyer.

"Harlan!" Amber said. "Knock it off."

Harlan wanted to take credit for moving the planchette, especially hearing the genuine unease in Amber's voice. But he hadn't done anything. He hadn't even been *thinking* about doing anything. He'd been glaring at Amber at the time.

The pointer jerked again.

"Harlan!" Amber said. "Stop!"

"I'm not doing it!" Harlan said, which was a mistake. Amber saw the look in his eyes. She knew he was telling the truth, that this wasn't the setup for some hilarious gag.

Then Harlan realized: if *he* wasn't moving the pointer and if *Amber* wasn't moving the pointer, who was?

No, he thought. That was crazy. Amber *had* to be moving it. What other explanation was there?

"It's moving!" someone said.

Sure enough, it was moving again, lurching awkwardly across the board. Everyone leaned forward at exactly the same time, even Ricky.

The pointer slid at an angle, toward the upper-right-hand corner, the one with the moon. It really did feel to Harlan like neither he nor Amber was moving it. But wasn't that what everyone said when they were using a Ouija board?

"It's heading for the 'No'!" Jerry said. He spoke the rest of his thought directly to Harlan. "Sorry, buddy, looks like there's no Oval Office in your future. But look at it this way—at least now you don't have to worry about how you spend your weekends in college!"

"It's not heading for the 'No,'" Rachel said. "It's stopping at the letters."

The pointer *was* stopping, in the middle of the lower arc of letters. It came to rest so it was pointing right between the "T" and the "U"—the Ouija board limbo between letters.

"What does that mean?" someone said.

"It's meaningless," someone else said. "Ask another question."

"Wait!" Rachel said. The pointer was sliding again, but not far, just to the upper row of letters.

"'H,'" Brian read. The pointer had stopped right at that letter. There was no mistaking it.

"'H' is for Harlan!" Jerry said.

"Which would make sense," Amber said, annoyed, "except for the fact that I asked it a yes-or-no question!" She talked down to the board: "Will Harlan ever be elected *president?*"

The pointer started moving again, but now it wasn't heading for either "Yes" or "No." It was heading down, toward the row of numbers near the base of the board.

"This isn't working," Amber said, looking away. "Maybe I need a new partner."

"Wait!" someone said. "It *is* working. It's stopping on a number."

"'Two,'" someone else said. "'H' and 'two.' Amber's right. That doesn't make any sense."

But the pointer was moving yet again, not herky-jerky this time, but smoothly, evenly. It was heading back to the letters.

Once again, everyone leaned in close.

"'O,'" someone read when it stopped again.

Amber looked back at the board. "Wait a minute," she said, thinking aloud. "'H_2O.' Water!"

"And Harlan's a swimmer!" Rachel said. "That's *it*!"

"Except it's still not the answer to the question I asked!" Amber sounded seriously peeved. And Harlan would have sworn that she had figured out the meaning of "H_2O" just then. Which meant that she wasn't moving the pointer, at least not consciously.

They were *both* moving the pointer. That was the answer; that's how a Ouija board worked. Harlan remembered that he'd read about it in a book somewhere. The two people with their fingers on the

61

pointer interacted with each other, each pushing it a little bit. The result was that it felt like neither one was really controlling it. But it was definitely the two people doing it. That's why a Ouija board didn't work when the players were blindfolded.

Except, Harlan realized, Amber hadn't even been looking at the pointer the last two times it stopped. Not only that, she was also reading the board upside down.

"Hey, Harlan," Jerry said. "You okay?"

"Huh?" Harlan said. He coughed. "Sure. Why?"

"You're being kinda quiet."

"No." Except that he *was* being quiet. Everyone in that room knew it.

Harlan was actually relieved when the pointer began moving again. This time it stopped on the 'D.'

"'D,'" someone said, even as it was moving again.

"'A,'" someone else said when it stopped.

"'N,'" someone said on the next letter.

"Water Dan?" Brian said. "Who's that?"

"Shhhh!" Rachel said. "It's still moving." She looked down at the board and read the next letter. "'G.'"

Harlan's heart skipped. He wasn't having a premonition. He just had a sense that whatever this Ouija board was spelling out, it wasn't good.

"'E,'" someone said.

"'R,'" someone else said.

"D-A-N-G-E-R," the board had spelled.

Danger!

"Danger?" Brian said.

"H_2O danger," Jerry said, and no one spoke for a second.

Harlan's pores were bursting with sweat—millions of tiny firecrackers exploding on his skin. Somehow he knew the message had something to do with his swimming.

"Well," Ricky said. "I guess the board's saying that if he runs for president, he'll definitely lose the mermaid vote!"

It wasn't a funny joke, but then, Ricky hadn't said it to get a laugh. He'd said it to break the tension of the room—and to remind Harlan just how silly this whole exercise was.

It worked. A couple of people laughed, and Jerry snorted. As for Harlan, the tension fell from his body like a heavy robe.

Harlan was a swimmer, and he and Amber had subconsciously spelled out the words "H_2O" and "danger" on a Ouija board. What was so strange about that? There were plenty of dangers in a swimming pool. Two years ago, a swimmer from Maple Park had dived into the shallow end, hit his head on the bottom, and almost ended up paralyzed.

"My fingers are cramping," Harlan said. "Someone else go." He shifted as if to lift his fingers from the planchette.

"Stop!" Amber barked. "We're not done!"

"What?" he said.

"It's still moving!" Amber said.

He glared at her. Why was she doing this? A minute ago she'd been annoyed that the Ouija board wasn't answering her question; now she wouldn't let him stop.

So why was he even listening to her? Why didn't he just pull his fingers from the pointer? But for some reason, her voice had commanded him, freezing his fingers on the plastic. And even as Harlan kept staring at her, the pointer slid an inch or so to the right and stopped again.

"'T,'" someone read.

It shifted to the next letter over.

"'U,'" someone else read.

Then, without warning, the pointer swept its way up and left, almost to the end of the upper arc of letters. It stopped suddenly, like it had caught on something, at exactly the spot to be pointing right at a letter. What were the odds of *that*?

"'B,'" someone read. "Tub."

And in an instant, Harlan realized what it was spelling.

Harriet Tubman High School. They had a swim meet there the following week.

H_2O danger Tub!

And suddenly Harlan saw himself in water. A premonition! But in his mind, he wasn't on top of the water, being supported by it. No, he was sinking into it. The water was washing over him, pulling him down. He was gasping for air, flailing, but it wasn't helping. Without warning, he sucked in a mouthful of water; it felt like someone jamming a solid rock down his throat. He continued to sink—and no one was coming to his rescue!

Harlan jerked his fingers from the pointer like he'd touched them on the burner of a stove. Somehow, the action also stopped the premonition in mid-image.

"Harlan!" Amber said. "What are you doing?"

"Nothing!" Harlan said, feeling himself flush. "I'm done! I told you, my fingers are cramping!"

"We're *not* done! The pointer was still moving! 'H_2O danger Tub'? That doesn't mean *anything!*"

"Well, you're definitely done now," Jerry said. "Once you take your fingers off the pointer, you break the spiritual connection."

Amber sighed. "Okay, so let's do it again."

"*No!*" Harlan said.

"Harlan—"

"*I'm not doing it!*" he shouted. "*You can't make me!*" Had he meant to slap the Ouija board like that? In any event, the board flipped up and the plastic pointer went flying across the room.

The room fell absolutely silent. Every eye was on him; even Ricky was too surprised to speak. Harlan knew that the only way to redeem himself in the eyes of Amber and their friends was to say something, make it seem like his outburst had been a joke.

But Harlan couldn't think of any jokes. He wouldn't have been able to choke the words out even if he had. And it wouldn't have mattered anyway—he saw that now. He was too pale, his breathing was too rapid. People had to see the panic in his eyes.

He just kept sitting there stupidly, with everyone staring right at him. At the same time, a car alarm went off somewhere on the street outside, and it caused the neighbors' dogs to start howling. It sounded like the baying of hungry wolves gathering for a kill.

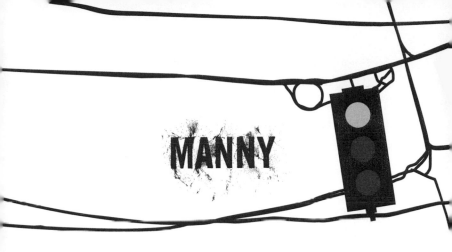

MANNY

The wooden stairs creaked under Manny's feet.

"Manny?" his dad said, below him in the basement. "Is that you?"

"Yeah," he said. "I'm coming down."

Talk to him, Manny thought. That's what Elsa had said. Talk to his dad. But what exactly would they talk *about*? That his dad had reacted strangely that one morning when Manny had told him about his nightmare? Maybe his dad really *had* remembered that he had some errands to run before work.

No. It was more than that. He'd been fine before Manny told him the dream. It was something about this particular dream—something Manny had said. It had meaning to his dad. There was something his dad wasn't telling him.

Manny found his dad in one corner of the basement,

rooting through a rack of cluttered metal shelves. The basement was unfinished, windowless, with walls of bare concrete; the air smelled of spray paint, Christmas spice, and dried aquarium mold.

"Hey," Manny said.

"Oh," his dad said. "Hello." The shelf had his attention, not Manny—not that that was necessarily such a bad thing.

"What are you doing?" Manny said. It seemed important to sound casual.

"Looking for some of that green florists' foam that you put at the bottom of a vase. You know, you poke flower stems in it so they'll stand upright? I was positive I had some."

"Let me help." Anything to avoid doing what he'd come down here to do. "Why do you need it?"

"Oh, I got snookered into donating something for this silent auction. I can't afford to actually buy anything, so I figured I'd make a flower arrangement." This was just like his dad—both the donation and the flower-arranging part. Knowing him, his arrangement would even turn out great.

His dad sighed and straightened. "Well, it's not here." He thought for a second, then glanced around the basement. "What else do we have that

I could fob off on the silent auction?"

"Dad?"

"Hmm?"

But Manny couldn't put into words what he was trying to say. He'd always been able to ask his dad anything. Why wasn't he able to ask him about this? Maybe because he wasn't even sure what he was asking.

"Planters," his dad said.

"Huh?" Manny said.

"We've got plenty of planters. Maybe I could fill one with tulips." He bent down to examine a cluster of ceramic pots. "Nah, they're all chipped. If they're not chipped, they're ugly. Why do I keep these plastic planters, anyway? I've never seen one that doesn't look cheap."

"I don't know," Manny said softly.

His dad kept scanning the clutter, thinking out loud. "Christmas is over, so wreaths and ornaments are out. I don't have time to reupholster furniture—not that any of our furniture is worth reupholstering anyway. Something to do with old CDs? A mobile or something?"

Manny just listened. What was he thinking—that the perfect segue would magically present itself? *Hey,*

Dad, speaking of mobiles, I wanted to ask you about breakfast the other morning. . . .

His dad sighed again. "I never realized what a load of junk we have. One of these days, we should take it to the dump. Well, I could always make fudge." He turned for the stairs.

"Wait!" Manny said.

His dad jumped a little, startled. "Manny? What is it?" He had his dad's full attention at last. But did he dare ask the question he wanted to ask?

Manny pointed. "The yard gnome! You could repaint it. Bright colors or something?"

No, Manny hadn't dared.

His dad cocked his head. "Well, it's a thought. But I think the crowd's going to be kind of upscale. Lots of lawyers." He started for the stairs again.

"Dad!" Manny said. "Wait."

His dad looked back at him again.

"There's something I want to ask," Manny said.

His dad's expression shifted. Was that nervousness Manny saw creeping across his face? Whatever it was, Manny was certain that his dad had suddenly realized what his son was going to ask.

"It's cold down here," his dad said, turning. "Can we talk about this upstairs?"

No, Manny thought, they couldn't talk about it

upstairs. If he didn't get this out now, he'd never be able to.

"Dad," he said. "The other day, at breakfast—"

"Breakfast?" his dad interrupted. "What are you talking about? Look, I've really got to get started on that fudge." Now Manny *knew* his dad had known what he was going to ask. He had responded far too quickly.

"Dad, just listen, okay?"

His dad stopped. He couldn't keep walking now, not without being really rude. But even so, he didn't turn around to face Manny again.

"It was when I was telling you about my nightmare," Manny said.

"I don't know what this has to do with—"

"It's just that you seemed kind of weird. And I thought maybe I said something that upset you."

"Upset me?" his dad said. "I don't have any idea what you're talking about."

"All of a sudden, you wanted to get away," Manny went on. "You said you had an errand to run before work, but I don't think you did."

His dad turned to him. "Manny, you were the one who was upset. You'd just had a nightmare!" So he *did* remember. He'd been lying before. And as Manny watched his dad now, he saw just how tightly he was gripping the rail at the base of the stairs.

"Are you sure?" Manny said. "Because it seemed like there was something else going on. I thought maybe my dream reminded you of something. Something about the past."

And right then, Manny knew: the nightmares were about something that had happened to him as a small child! He wasn't sure how he knew this, but he did.

"Saturday!" his dad said suddenly.

"What?" Manny was confused.

"That's when we're throwing all this stuff away! I'll call Goodwill! Maybe they can send a truck! Now, Manny, I've really got to get started on that fudge." Then, without another word, he thundered up the stairs.

This time, Manny let him go. It didn't matter. There was nothing he could say to get his dad to give him a straight answer.

Which was, of course, an answer of sorts.

Manny stared at his dad's address book. He'd had the same one for as long as Manny could remember, and it looked like it, dog-eared and doodled on. His dad was always misplacing the damn thing, but Manny had found it right away, by the phone in the kitchen, in the clutter of coupons and utility bills.

Manny thought for a second. Whatever his dad wasn't telling him had something to do with Manny's childhood, something that had happened to him when he was younger. So there had to be someone he could ask about that past: an uncle or an old family friend who could answer the questions that his dad would not, maybe even some relatives of his dead mother.

Manny kept staring at that closed address book, but no names came to mind. Not a single one. He couldn't think of anyone who might be able to tell him what he wanted to know. His dad said his own family was all gone: he'd never had any siblings, and his parents and grandparents had all died before Manny was born—Manny had never asked how. As for relatives of his dead mom, his dad had never once mentioned any. Could it really be that his dad had lost all contact with them?

And even if his dad's relatives were all dead, where were his childhood friends? His college roommate? Sure, his dad had moved since then, but didn't he keep a Christmas card list? But there *were* no old family friends, not that Manny could think of.

He started paging through the address book.

Henry Bean. Jason Berg. Ernie Cruz.

Mostly single fathers, Manny saw. That made sense. Birds of a feather. No one in the address book was scratched out completely—that was the kind of person his father was, never expunging anyone from his life forever. But plenty of addresses and phone numbers had been updated—crossed out and replaced by newer addresses and phone numbers squeezed into the margins.

Jamie Gardner. Margaret Graham. Katie Ingram.

These were women his dad had dated; even though none of his relationships had ever worked out, he'd stayed friends with some of them. Once he'd overheard one of them accuse his dad of having "issues." At the time, he'd thought she was just being overbearing. But now, given the way his dad had reacted to the nightmare, Manny thought maybe that ex-girlfriend had had a point.

Larry Middle. Sarah Newman. Matthew Orner.

Some of his dad's friends had moved six or seven times in the years that his father had kept this book, mostly from apartment to apartment. It looked more like the address book of a college student. But it was really just the result of most of his dad's friends' being just as poor as they were.

Melinda Walker. Eldon Wood. Tim Yates.

He had come to the end of the address book. He

closed it and put it back on the counter.

He had recognized every single name. He also knew exactly where and when his dad had met them all: each and every one in the last thirteen years that they'd lived in this city.

The address book was old, but apparently it wasn't more than thirteen years old.

There was no one Manny could ask. It was as if the past, at least the past before they moved to their current city, did not exist.

For the first time in his life, Manny realized that that was pretty damn suspicious.

Manny went for a long walk in the fading afternoon sun. The idea had been to clear his mind, but it sure wasn't working. On the contrary, a tornado of questions swirled through his head. Why didn't his dad have a past? Had his dad been estranged from his parents? Is that why he didn't keep any pictures of them? Had they disowned him? Were they still alive? Where had Manny and his dad moved from, anyway—and why hadn't his dad ever said? Where did Manny's dead mother fit into all of this? And, of course, he still had the question that had started it all: What was it about his nightmare that was causing his dad to act so strangely?

Something had happened when Manny was a child. That had been his first thought. But what could possibly explain all the mysteries that had suddenly surfaced about his dad's past?

Was it something that had happened *to* Manny? Maybe the event that explained his dad's odd behavior was also the event that was causing Manny's nightmares. Maybe he had long-buried memories that were finally reemerging in the form of dreams. If it was something his dad was trying to keep hidden, that would certainly explain his strange behavior in the kitchen and basement.

Manny caught something out of the corner of his eye—a handwritten sign in the front window of a small beige house.

Marilyn Swan, it read. *Spiritual Reader.*

Manny looked around. He had wandered into an older residential area—the kind with postage-stamp yards and streets that still had sidewalks and curbs.

He looked back at the house with the sign. It had window boxes and a stucco finish. There was a bird-bath in the yard—made of real stone, something his dad would approve of, not Home Depot plastic. And the lawn was well edged, and cut as low as a putting green.

Manny was actually considering going to a psychic?

A couple of weeks ago, if someone had told him to go to a psychic, he would have laughed. And yet here he was. He desperately needed answers, and there was no one else who was able to give them to him. He knew she was probably a fraud. Maybe he just needed someone to talk to, someone to help him sort out his thoughts. Either way, how could it possibly hurt?

He walked down a narrow concrete pathway that curved its way to the front door. Then he knocked.

A moment later, the door opened. Could this be Marilyn Swan? She was an older woman, primly but tastefully dressed, a well-heeled matron expecting the Ladies' Auxiliary for tea. Her smile was honey and molasses, sprinkled with powered sugar.

"Uh, hi," Manny said. "I have some questions, and I was wondering if you'd—"

"I'm so sorry," she said, projecting sincerity like heat from a radiator. "Unfortunately, I'm with a client right now. But if you'd like to come back later . . ." She handed him a business card in a tasteful font, no rainbows, no angels, nothing froufrou at all. "It really is best to make an appointment."

And with that, she smiled again and closed the door in his face.

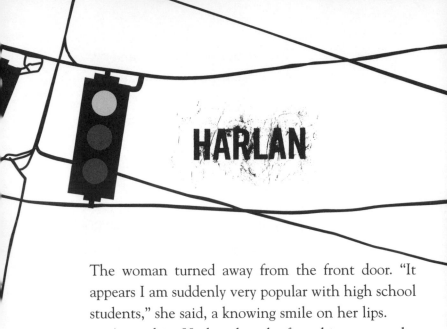

HARLAN

The woman turned away from the front door. "It appears I am suddenly very popular with high school students," she said, a knowing smile on her lips.

A psychic, Harlan thought from his seat on the sofa in the woman's living room. He'd actually come to get a "spiritual reading" from a psychic. What if the press found out? His mom would be livid. She'd specifically warned him to stay away from psychics; apparently Nancy Reagan had caught hell for consulting with psychics when she was First Lady.

On the other hand, if premonitions and Ouija boards told the truth, maybe psychics did too.

"Now, where were we?" said the woman—Marilyn Swan, according to the sign in her window. "Ah, yes. Do you take lemon in your tea?" She lowered herself into a seat in front of the tea set on the coffee table.

Harlan didn't take anything in his tea, mostly because he didn't take tea. But he said, "Yes, please."

"So," she said. "Tell me how I can help you." She had poured two cups of tea before she'd answered that knock on the front door; now she squeezed lemon into them both.

"It's kind of complicated," Harlan said.

"It usually is. That's why I believe it's always best to start at the very beginning. Sugar?"

"No, thank you." He watched her drop a cube of sugar into her own cup and stir. "I'm sorry," he said. "Maybe this is rude, but I can't help asking. How did you become a spiritual reader?"

"I don't seem like the typical psychic, is that it?"

"Not exactly." Then, thinking that maybe he'd offended her, he added, "I'm not sure what I expected."

She handed him his tea. "It started when my husband, Richard, died."

"I'm sorry."

"Thank you. My, you're such a polite young man. Anyway, the night of the funeral, I came home and found him sitting in his favorite chair, just like usual." She nodded to a black leather wing chair with matching footrest just opposite her. "He was as real as you are."

"A ghost?"

"For lack of a better word. For a long time, I thought I was imagining things. And I knew what other people would say, so I didn't dare tell anyone. But then Richard started telling me things. Things about other people, things I didn't know but that turned out to be true."

"He could predict the future?"

She sipped her tea. "Sometimes he sees the future, but mostly he sees the past. But you'd be surprised how, for most people, the past and the future are very much the same thing. Cookie?"

"No, thank you."

"Anyway, it seems that in Richard's past, he had made some rather poor business decisions. He told me about them too, even though by then it was too late to do anything about them. Before long, I was broke, or near enough. I needed to get a job, but suffice it to say that there was not a large demand for a fifty-six-year-old housewife who could not process words. Then, one day, Richard suggested that I become a spiritual reader. He said he could tell me what to say. Of course, my friends were horribly shocked. Then they heard what Richard had to say. They're all clients now."

"What are you saying?" Harlan said. "Richard is still here?"

"That's right."

"He's here right now?"

She nodded, the knowing little smile back on her lips.

Harlan looked over at the empty wing chair, then sat upright in his own seat.

Mrs. Swan kept smiling. "People always do that. When I tell them there's a ghost in the room, they always sit up straighter. As if somehow a ghost would expect them to have better posture."

"I . . ." Harlan didn't know what to say. Until recently, he had *always* known what to say.

"So," Marilyn Swan said. "How can we help you?"

"We," Harlan thought. She had actually said "we." Was she serious? He looked at her, sipping tea and watching him.

She was certifiable. Of course she was! He hadn't known what to expect by coming to a psychic, but it sure wasn't taking tea with Lady Properly and her dead husband. Maybe it was like what everyone said about hot dogs—that they tasted all right, but you really didn't want to know how they were made. Well, Harlan had seen inside Mrs. Swan's slaughterhouse, and now he didn't want any more of her hot dogs.

"You know," he said, standing, "I just remembered

how much homework I have to do. I really should get going." He reached for his wallet. "I'll pay you for your time, of course."

Mrs. Swan sat quietly for a moment. Then she looked up at Harlan and said, "Richard wants to know about the party."

Harlan froze. "What?"

"A party. Something happened at a party. He says that's the reason you're here."

Harlan stared at her. Had he mentioned Jerry's party when he came in? No, he was certain he hadn't.

He looked over at the empty wing chair. Then he put his wallet away and sat back down.

He took a sip of tea. Finally he said, softly, "It was a Ouija board. It spelled something." He wasn't sure where to look—at Mrs. Swan or the wing chair. So he looked down at his feet. Then he told Mrs. Swan what the Ouija board had spelled. H_2O *danger Tub.*

"I'm a swimmer," he went on. "And I have a swim meet on Wednesday. At Harriet Tubman High School. I think that's what the Ouija board was talking about." He looked up at her at last. "What's going to happen if I go to that swim meet?"

Mrs. Swan was quiet for a moment; then she nodded, though Harlan wasn't sure if she was nodding at him or her husband. "As I said, Richard's forte isn't necessarily the future. Besides, he usually doesn't put much stock in Ouija boards."

"'Usually'? What about when things aren't usual?"

Mrs. Swan smiled. "Richard likes you. He thinks you're smart."

"Mrs. Swan, please."

She listened to Richard, then said, "Dark forces, just like people say. Evil spirits from foul dimensions. But for such a force to inhabit this world, to speak through a Ouija board, it must be connected to a person. These dark forces need our essences to be anchored here; otherwise they get swept back to where they came from. So they attach to our souls. Sort of spiritual stowaways. But they can only attach to a wounded or confused soul—someone who is so disoriented, he or she doesn't recognize the presence of the dark force alongside his or her own. For a dark force to have spoken to you through a Ouija board, it would have to be connected to you."

Harlan waited for her to say the rest: that there was no dark force connected to him. Because that's what she meant, right? His soul wasn't "wounded" or "confused." But if that's what she meant, why wasn't she saying it?

"Anyway," Mrs. Swan said. "This isn't the beginning.

Richard thinks we should start at the beginning."

So Harlan took a breath and told her—them?—about the premonitions: about the choking, the drowning, and all the rest. And about how he'd seen an image of himself being hit by a vehicle, and then how a bus had almost run him over at the corner of Grand and Humble.

"So one premonition *did* come true—or almost," Mrs. Swan said. "But the premonitions haven't stopped."

"Yes," Harlan said. That was it exactly.

"But that's not the beginning," Mrs. Swan said.

"What isn't?"

"The premonitions. That's not when all this really began. It began before the premonitions. With an accident."

"What kind of accident? I haven't been in any accident."

"Long ago."

Harlan thought for a second. When he was twelve, he'd had a big wipeout on his skateboard. But he was sure that wasn't what she was talking about.

"In the water," Mrs. Swan said.

Harlan perked up. "Water?" H_2O *danger Tub!* "But that's what the Ouija board said! That I'm in danger if I go to that swim meet!"

"As I mentioned," Mrs. Swan said, "the past and the future are often one and the same. They can also be very hard to distinguish. Especially for a soul in turmoil."

"What are you saying? That my soul is confused?" He didn't say out loud the rest of what he was thinking: that if his soul was confused, then there *could* be dark forces stowing away on his essence!

She tilted her head, listening. "Richard says there was an accident in the water. It wasn't your fault, but you almost died. And that's when things started to go wrong."

"Wrong? What do you mean?"

"Your life's road. Your spiritual direction. You've been led astray, to a dead end. That's why you see death. You're doomed to repeat the tragedy of the past until you get back on the right spiritual road."

"What road? What tragedy?"

"Stop it!" Mrs. Swan almost shouted. "I'm sorry," she said to Harlan, more softly but perspiring. "You're both talking at once. It's confusing me."

Harlan waited breathlessly for her to speak again, for her to tell him how Richard thought he could get back on the right spiritual road. But instead of speaking, Mrs. Marilyn Swan reached for a cookie from the plate in front of her.

That was when Harlan knew: she was a fraud after all. It was the cookie that had done it. Here she was, supposedly all flustered from the different "voices," and she'd reached for a cookie? A drink of tea he would have bought—some liquid to soothe her ragged throat. But people didn't eat in the midst of a real emotional disturbance.

He thought about all that she had told him so far. That something happened at a party? That could have been a lucky guess; good-looking teenagers like Harlan were always going to parties. And since parties meant lots of people, that meant lots of chances for her to stumble upon some important interaction of his. Then there was the "accident in the water." How vague was that? And besides, he'd just told her what the Ouija board had spelled out.

H_2O *danger Tub*.

She had just taken the little bit of information he'd given her, rearranged it, and repeated it back to him to make it sound like she was saying something real.

Her act had been a good one—especially the bit with her serving tea, and the dead husband. And she'd performed it impressively—well enough for it to be worth the price he would pay for it, to tell the truth. He had almost been convinced. But it *had* been an act. He was sure of that now. At least he had realized the truth before she had made him do something stupid—or bilked him out of a lot of money.

"That's funny," Mrs. Swan said to herself. She still hadn't taken a bite of the cookie in her hand.

"What is?" Harlan asked.

"Richard is gone." She dropped the cookie back on the plate; it landed with a clink and broke into pieces. Then she glanced around the room. "Richard?"

"Maybe he stepped out for a minute," Harlan said, starting to stand again. "And I think that I should—"

"You don't understand. Richard has never left before!" Her eyes had gone wild; her jaw had become a junction of creases and tremors.

She was an incredible actress. She should be doing theater, Harlan thought, except it probably didn't pay as well.

Suddenly Mrs. Swan stood up from her chair. Her leg caught the corner of the tea tray, knocking it over. Nothing broke, but everything spilled—milk, tea, and sugar, all over the carpet.

"Mrs. Swan?"

She didn't say a word. She ignored the spilled tea and milk, just let it soak into the carpet. She stood there, hunched down and glaring around the room like a cat before an earthquake.

"What is it?"

"There's something here with us!" she hissed. "Not Richard!"

Harlan smiled. Here it goes. There were "dark forces" stowing away on his "confused" soul after all. And of course only Mrs. Swan was going to be able to banish them—for a not inconsequential price, of course. He marveled at how cleverly it had all been set up.

But to Harlan's surprise, she didn't ask him for money. Instead, she said, "You must go!" Without waiting for a response, she stepped closer to him but stopped short, like she was afraid to actually touch him. "Please! You must leave!"

"Wait," Harlan said. "Don't you have something to banish the dark forces?"

"What? No! Now go!"

"But the money I owe you—"

"No! Just go! And please don't come back!"

"Don't come back"? Harlan thought. But if he didn't come back, how was she going to scam him out of his money?

"Mrs. Swan. . . ?"

Now she *was* touching him, roughly, prodding him toward the door but still trying to keep her hands off him as much as possible, like she had just learned he had leprosy. "Go!" she said. "You must go!"

Okay, now he was confused. What sort of con *was* this? Did she ruin her carpet for all her dupes? Was she able to conjure up such a convincing fear in her eyes for everyone?

They reached the door, and she threw it open. "I'm sorry!" she said. Even before he could respond, she tried to push him through.

He caught himself on the doorframe. "Wait!" he said. "At least tell me what to do! To get rid of the dark forces? I'll do anything you want!" This was what she wanted, right? For him to plead with her? For him to be willing to spend any amount of money? Because this *was* all a con; it had to be! Because if it wasn't—

Mrs. Swan shoved him through the door.

"Mrs. Swan "

She slammed the door in his face.

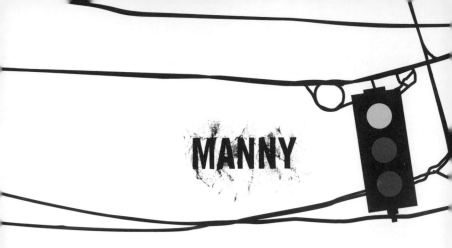

MANNY

Manny stood in the bridge of the original U.S. starship *Enterprise*. The door had just swooshed closed behind him.

"Captain." Mr. Spock spoke to Manny from his place at the science officer's station. "I'm picking up some kind of large astral body up ahead."

"On-screen," Manny said, crossing to the captain's chair, where he took his seat. But as he sat, something crunched underneath him. He stood up again and looked down to see that he'd crushed a pair of wire-rim spectacles.

He ignored the spectacles and glanced up at the viewscreen, which now revealed a large swath of deep space. In the middle of the screen was a great ice-encrusted asteroid barreling right at them.

"I don't like the look of *that*!" Dr. McCoy said

from a seat next to Manny's.

"According to my calculations," Mr. Spock said, "we are on a direct collision course with the asteroid."

"Evasive maneuvers, Mr. Sulu," Manny said.

Mr. Sulu, sitting at the helm, punched helplessly at the controls. "I'm sorry, Captain," he said. "The controls are not responding." He sniffed the air. "Does anyone else smell gasoline?"

Manny hit a button in the armrest of the captain's chair; it activated an intercom to the Engine Room. "Dad?" he said. "Are you there?"

There was no answer.

"Dad!"

"Engine Room here," said a voice. It was a man, but it was definitely not his father.

"You're not my dad," Manny said.

"Yes, I am," said the voice.

"No, you're not!"

"Captain," Mr. Spock said. "Logic would dictate that it does not matter at this point whether the man in the Engine Room is your actual genetic forebear."

Manny agreed. "We've lost control of the helm!" he said to the Engine Room. "Can you get us back online?"

There was a moment's hesitation. Then the voice

said, "No." And with that, Manny and the U.S.S. *Enterprise* slammed right into the ice-encrusted asteroid.

So did you talk to him? Elsa signed eagerly.

Manny nodded.

And? Elsa said. *What did he say?*

That he couldn't get the helm back online, Manny thought. And as a result, we'd crashed into the ice-encrusted asteroid. Oh, Manny remembered, and he also wasn't my dad.

He and Elsa were standing in the hallway before class. Manny had another headache, and his eyesight was as blurry as ever. But Elsa was staring at him, waiting for an answer.

He was even weirder than before, Manny said. *There's definitely something he's not telling me. I think it's something that happened to me as a kid.*

What makes you think that?

A feeling. But I'm sure of it.

So that's it! The movie's off! Suddenly, Elsa's signs were fast and wide.

Why?

Because now we have a new project: we have to find out what happened to you when you were a kid!

Really? Manny said.

Are you kidding? Now I'm just as curious as you!

The stairs still creaked on the way down to the basement. But this time Manny wasn't dreading what was at the bottom of those stairs; this time he was eager to get to the bottom—of the stairs, and of whatever the hell it was that was causing his nightmares.

Why down here? Elsa signed at the base of the stairs. *Why not start looking in your dad's bedroom?*

It's just another feeling I have, Manny said. *I think there's something down here—a clue or something.*

In the light of the bare bulb overhead, they stared at all the clutter piled haphazardly up against the concrete walls—folding chairs, an old sewing machine, the croquet set, lawn furniture, a table leaf, a computer monitor, and several shopping bags full of wire coat hangers. There were also plenty of cardboard boxes.

Neither Manny nor Elsa said anything for a second. A big brown spider darted across the floor, a nimble cluster of long legs desperate for shelter from the light. But halfway across the concrete, the spider stopped, and Manny realized that it was hunting, not running, and that it had captured some kind of prey.

It's hard to look for something when you don't know

what you're looking for, Elsa signed.

You're not kidding, Manny said.

Since he had to start somewhere, he knelt down in front of the closest cardboard box. He opened it and found it was full of snapshots, which seemed promising. They were all still in the envelopes from the developing lab (his dad couldn't afford a digital camera). But what was Manny supposed to do now— sort through them all?

Look, it's our Egyptian sarcophagus! Elsa was pointing to a rounded wooden casket standing upright in one corner of the basement. Its gold paint and colorful Egyptian imagery had been dulled by time and dust, but it was still an impressive sight. *Remember when we found it at that theater's old prop sale? We have to use it in a movie!*

Manny looked down at the photos in the cardboard box. The envelopes all came from the same developing lab—the same place that his dad had been taking their film ever since they'd moved to town thirteen years ago. There weren't any unfamiliar envelopes—which meant that there weren't any photos more than thirteen years old either, baby pictures or the like.

Where *did* his dad keep those? Now that he thought about it, he couldn't remember *ever* seeing a picture of himself as a baby. Was that possible? It couldn't be the case that his dad hadn't taken any photos of him; he always took lots of photos.

Elsa's gesticulating hands caught his attention again. *Look at this!* she was saying. She'd found her and Manny's papier-mâché dinosaur from the sixth grade—a six-foot-long blue *Brontosaurus* with a long, sweeping neck. *Do you remember how much work this was? It was this stupid neck! Remember how it kept breaking? We'd finish it, get it all dried and painted, and then it would break. See? It's broken now. It's your fault. I wanted to make a* Tyrannosaurus rex!

Everyone wanted to make a Tyrannosaurus rex," Manny signed to her. He opened another box and saw it contained kitchen utensils—measuring cups and spoons, wire whisks, a scum-encrusted blender—and an old-fashioned jack in the box. So much for his dad's organizational skills.

This was such a disappointment, Elsa went on, still meaning the dinosaur. *When you're a kid, nothing ever turns out as good as you imagine.*

Manny spotted an old seaman's chest up against the wall near Elsa. He was pretty sure it was full of winter clothes—snow pants, wool socks, stuff like that—but he wanted to make sure.

He motioned to Elsa. *Try that chest, would you?*

95

But she wasn't watching him now. She'd found a cardboard box of her own. *It's the decorations from our haunted house!* she signed, barely looking at him. *Remember trying to figure out how to turn those wig-rests into decapitated heads? Paint kept dissolving the Styrofoam. We ended up using my mom's makeup, right?*

Elsa! he repeated. *That chest?*

And here's our skeleton! she went on. *We had to mail-order this, didn't we? But it sure looked good. Imagine if we'd had to use one of those paper skeletons!*

Manny walked over to her and yanked her sleeve. *Forget the* damn *Halloween decorations! Would you remember why we're here?*

She stared at him like he'd slapped her. He hadn't said anything out loud, but he'd yelled at her all the same. He had never been so angry with her before, and he knew the anger was still right there on his face.

Elsa was so surprised that her face lost all expression. Looking at her now reminded him of staring into a deep lake whose surface had suddenly stilled so he could see all the way to the bottom. There were strange shapes down there, confusing forms—feelings of Elsa's that Manny didn't know were there and, even now, he couldn't quite identify.

I'm sorry, she said quickly, her hands uncharacteristically clumsy. *Manny, I'm really sorry!* As fast as it had calmed, the surface of the lake had rippled over again. To tell the truth, Manny was glad that the clear view into her soul was gone.

He shook his head. *No, I'm sorry. I shouldn't have snapped at you. I'm not sure why I did.* Where *had* that anger come from? It had popped up out of nowhere like—well, like a jack-in-the-box.

He walked back to the cardboard box to look at the toy nestled in with the kitchen utensils. It was a wooden jack-in-the-box with a dulled brass crank. Each side of the box had been carved and painted with a different letter—a blue "M," for example, and a red "H."

It was his. He used to play with it as a boy. He hadn't seen it for years, had forgotten all about it. But it was coming back to him now. There was something unusual that popped up from inside—not a clown, something else.

It wasn't surprising that his dad had saved his old jack-in-the-box. From the look of it, it was pretty valuable. Besides, his dad saved everything—every snapshot, every kitchen utensil, even every wire coat hanger, apparently. Except that wasn't quite true, was it? He hadn't saved any of Manny's other toys. No baby pictures, and no toys.

He looked around the basement and saw he was right. And it wasn't just toys. His dad hadn't saved any evidence of Manny's early years at all—no trike, no crib, no bassinet. Nothing from before their move thirteen years ago. It was as if Manny had never *been* a baby, as if he'd crawled almost fully formed from some kind of pod. What was that about? Manny knew the answer his dad would give: he'd thrown everything away when they'd moved thirteen years ago.

Except for the jack-in-the-box. It was beautiful—a work of art. Hand-carved, no doubt.

Elsa watched him watching it. *What is it?* she asked.

I'm not sure, he signed. He reached for the toy.

It was heavier than he expected. He needed to turn the crank. If he could get the thing to open, see the inside, then he'd know—not just what was inside the jack-in-the-box, but maybe also whatever it was that had happened to him as a child that was causing his nightmares.

And yet he hesitated before turning the crank. Did he want to know the truth or not?

There was a creak at the top of the stairs. "Manny? Are you down there?"

His dad! He'd come home! How had Manny not heard him come in? He'd been distracted, first by Elsa, then by the jack-in-the-box.

"Yeah," he said, not loudly, not softly. "I'm here." The door was open and the light was on, so it wasn't like he could lie.

Manny heard footsteps—loud ones, more urgent than they should have been. The stairs didn't squeak now; they trembled. Manny stood up, still holding the jack-in-the-box. Without thinking, he slipped the toy behind his back.

Halfway down the steps, his dad said, "What are you doing down here?" It was more than a question, but not quite an accusation. He stopped when he saw Elsa, but he didn't greet her yet. No, he wanted an answer from Manny.

Manny needed a lie, and he needed one quick.

"Going through our stuff," he said, mustering up all the innocence he could manage. "Why wouldn't I? Didn't you say that we're taking it all to Goodwill?" Realizing how stiff he looked trying to hide the jack-in-the-box behind his back, Manny forced himself to relax.

At the bottom of the stairs now, his dad looked at him, then glanced quickly around the basement. When he didn't see anything out of the ordinary, he finally looked at Elsa and smiled, saying, "Hi, Elsa."

Hello, Elsa signed.

His dad looked back at Manny, thinking. Then he

smiled again, as if he'd made up his mind about something.

"What?" Manny said.

His dad shook his head. "Nothing. I'll make dinner." And he turned for the steps.

As his dad started climbing back up the steps, Manny looked down at the jack-in-the-box, which he'd pulled part of the way out from behind his back. He could hardly wait for his dad to leave so he could open it up.

But at that exact second, a third of the way up the stairs, his dad suddenly turned back around. "Manny, did you happen to—?" He stopped, eyes locked on Manny—and on whatever it was he was holding down at his side. "What do you have there?"

"What?" Manny said. Suddenly it was deer-in-the-headlights time. It would only make things worse to now try to hide the jack-in-the-box again; on the other hand, he still didn't want to show his dad what he'd found. So he just stood there, frozen, looking tense and very, very guilty. "It's nothing," Manny said, trying—now unsuccessfully—to sound casual. "Just something I found in one of these boxes."

"What *is* it?" his dad said. He was trying hard to sound casual too, but he wasn't any more convincing than Manny had been.

And already he was starting down the creaking stairs.

Manny had no choice but to show his dad the jack-in-the-box. "It's a toy," Manny said. "I found it in with the kitchen stuff."

His dad stopped in front of Manny, eyes on the jack-in-the-box like it was a ticking time bomb about to explode.

"Can I see it?" his dad said.

"Huh?" Manny said. "Oh, I guess." He handed it over, forcing himself to do it nonchalantly.

"Hey!" his dad said, holding the toy. "I just got a great idea!"

Right then, Manny knew he would never hold that jack-in-the-box, or even see it, ever again.

"What?" Manny said meekly.

"I can donate this old jack-in-the-box to the silent auction! I mean, it's in great shape. And it's obviously a classic. It just needs a little restoring."

"But—" Manny knew there was nothing he could say. Even if he protested—if he told his dad he wanted to save the jack-in-the-box because it was the only childhood toy he had left—his dad would just say something about how important it was for the charity. No matter what Manny said, his dad was taking that jack-in-the-box. He couldn't even tell him to hold on a minute, ask his dad to let him turn the crank just one last time. His dad wouldn't let him. He would make some excuse. And Manny couldn't go to the silent auction and turn the crank either, because it wouldn't be there. That jack-in-the-box was being swept out of his life forever, and there was nothing whatsoever Manny could do about it.

Manny's dad was already halfway up the stairs with the toy. "Why don't you ask Elsa if she wants to stay for dinner?" he called back. "I'm making lentil tacos." And as quickly as he had appeared, he and the jack-in-the-box were gone.

Manny looked over at Elsa. She stared at him. To her credit, she looked as if she'd understood the essence of what had just happened. This was a good thing, because Manny was absolutely certain that he did not.

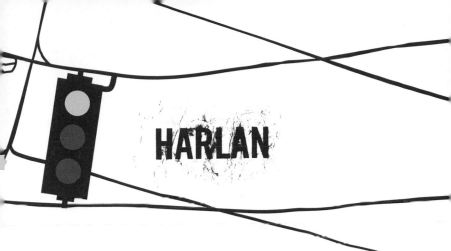

HARLAN

Harlan desperately needed to breathe; he just couldn't hold his breath any longer. He swung his head to one side and gasped for air. It helped, but only for a second. A second later, he needed to breathe again.

It was swim practice that Thursday, and once again he was swimming side by side with Ricky. He had skipped the swim meet at Harriet Tubman High School the day before. He'd told the coach he was sick, but of course that wasn't the real reason he hadn't gone.

H_2O danger Tub!

Sure, the message from the Ouija board was probably just random words, or something conjured up from his own subconscious. But he couldn't chance it—especially not after that bizarre encounter with the psychic, Marilyn Swan.

Even so, the premonitions had not stopped. He was still seeing—and experiencing—visions of his future death. In one, he'd been trapped on a sinking ship, water gushing in around him. In another, he'd seen himself lying on his back in a cold alley, being pummeled in the chest by an enormous thug. He had avoided whatever might have happened at Harriet Tubman High School—but new dangers had materialized to replace that one, like a whole range of mountains rising up on the horizon after the first peak had been passed.

And now his swimming was crap. For one thing, his breathing completely sucked. His intake was way down, and his rhythm was just plain *off*.

There was a reason, of course. That afternoon, during World History, Harlan had finally found a way to stave off the premonitions, or so it seemed; he had forced himself to focus on the here and now, concentrating on every aspect of the present, everything he was thinking and feeling. Marilyn Swan had said that "dark forces" stayed in this world by latching onto the soul of a person who did not notice them. Harlan didn't believe that, not really. But maybe part of him did, because it somehow made sense that if he was totally conscious of every thought and feeling, there wouldn't be anywhere for the dark forces to hide, nothing for them to hold on to. In any event, being totally self-aware had stopped the premonitions, at least for now.

But it had come at a cost. He hadn't had a premonition since World History, true, but by concentrating on everything, he couldn't concentrate on any *one* thing, like his swimming. He had to tell himself to kick, to stroke, to turn and push off from the wall. But that meant there couldn't be any merging of mind and body now, no spiritual connection with Ricky swimming next to him. On the contrary, he barely even felt a connection to his own body. It was like he was outside himself; his mind was still attached to his body, but it was as if it was being dragged behind, like an ocean mine on a metal chain. It was all he could do to keep from drowning.

Drowning. That reminded him of another thing Marilyn Swan had said. That he'd had an "accident" in water. It couldn't be true. Like everything else she'd said, it was just so much bullshit. So why did it *feel* so true? Why did he imagine he could feel the water closing in over him? Why did it feel like if he didn't immediately turn his head and take another breath, he'd inhale a mouthful of water? Because he'd psyched himself out, that's why.

The set ended at last. Harlan and Ricky sat in the

water at the end of their lane, fingers on their neck arteries, staring at the big overhead clock and measuring their pulses.

"One sixty," Ricky said at last. He looked at Harlan.

"Same," Harlan lied. His pulse had really been 200, but that wasn't bad when you considered that these days his resting pulse was probably barely under 130.

"All right, folks!" called the coach from the door of his pool office. "Let's run some sprints! Everyone down to the starting blocks."

"I'm not doing it!" said Jerry Blain from two lanes over, wildly splashing and flailing his arms. "You can't make me!" Except for Ricky, the whole pool laughed, and Harlan knew this was a reference to what he'd said at Jerry's party on Saturday night, the way he'd reacted when Amber had asked him to put his hands back on the Ouija board. By now, the whole school knew what had happened.

Everyone looked to Harlan, figuring he'd have some sort of comeback, still expecting the true alpha male to somehow put Jerry in his place. But Harlan didn't know what to say. For one thing, he had such a firm grip on his emotions that he worried that giving in to his anger at Jerry would cause his whole tightly wound existence to unravel.

"What's the matter, Chesterton?" Jeremy Ferber said. "Ghost got your tongue?"

"Watch it, Ferber," Ricky said. "He can still kick *your* butt." Ricky turned to Harlan. "Just ignore 'em." He adjusted the goggles on his head. "Come on, let's swim to the starting blocks."

Harlan stared down at the water; even now, it seemed to press in on him. "You know, it's not really happening for me today. I think I'll check out early." Then he climbed out of the pool and headed for the relative safety of the locker room.

"They're idiots," Ricky said.

It was a couple of minutes later, in the locker room. Harlan was getting dressed. Ricky stood at the far end of the row of lockers, still in his suit and dripping from the pool.

"Whatever," Harlan said.

"They're just jealous that you're so much better than they are," Ricky said.

Harlan wasn't completely dry, but he stepped into his pants anyway. "It's not just the guys on the team," he said. "It's the whole school. I made a fool out of myself, and no one's going to let me forget it."

Ricky stepped closer, clutching his own biceps in an effort to ward off the chill of the locker room.

"They'll forget it just as soon as you do. That's what they're reacting to, you know. Something in you. The old Harlan never would've let people say stuff like that."

"Maybe not." Harlan buttoned his shirt.

"So?"

"So what?"

"So what's goin' on?"

Harlan didn't say anything, just sat down on the bench to put on his socks and shoes.

"Come on, Har. Talk to me."

"It's nothing. I'm fine." But Harlan had said it too fast. It sounded defensive, not at all convincing.

Ricky crouched down to Harlan's level and lowered his voice. "Come on, man, what's wrong? You really think there's anything you can't tell *me*?"

But Harlan was already done with his shoes. He stood up again. He crammed his wet suit, goggles, and towel into his pack and turned for the exit.

"There's nothing wrong," he said, starting for the door. "I'll see you around, okay?"

Inside the school theater, the stage lights were on full, with the cast of *Camelot* in the middle of a rehearsal. But Harlan knew that meant no one on-stage could see back to the last row of the theater, where he took a seat. He could hear floorboards squeaking behind him—someone was moving around up in the lighting booth—but if anyone asked why Harlan was there, he could just say he was waiting for Amber, who was up onstage with the cast.

Why had Harlan come here? To think? He was tired of thinking. Maybe it was just to get away, to be somewhere where no one would bother him. Why hadn't he been able to tell Ricky what was on his mind? He knew Ricky wouldn't judge. But he just couldn't bring himself to say out loud all the things he'd been thinking and feeling.

"Sorry!" said a voice. "I did not know you were there." Someone was in the aisle next to him in the theater, someone who'd come to take a seat in the back row just like he had. But the voice sounded strange, atonal.

It was a girl from his class. He could see her clearly because light shone in from the lobby.

"I know you," he said. "Elsa." They'd never talked, but you didn't get to be student body president without knowing everyone in school. So the first month of every year, he went through the school phone directory and memorized the name of every kid, just like his mom had told him to. Elsa was deaf, but she read lips. But Harlan knew Sign, so he motioned to her with his hands. *I didn't know you could talk.*

She stared at him. *I didn't know you knew Sign!* she responded.

Even now, Harlan had to admit he liked surprising people. *I work with deaf kids*, he signed. *At the YMCA.* What Harlan didn't say was that he'd learned ASL because his mom thought photos or footage of a politician signing always made great press. But he definitely had an aptitude for the language—so much so that lately, while talking to the kids at the Y, he'd even caught himself "thinking" in Sign.

You waiting for someone? she asked him.

He nodded up toward the stage. *My girlfriend. Amber Hodges.*

Elsa smiled. *I know who your girlfriend is.*

Of course she knows, Harlan thought. Everyone knows who I am, and everyone knows who my girlfriend is. Harlan wondered if even Elsa—The Deaf Girl—had heard what had happened at the party on Saturday night.

You waiting for someone too? Harlan asked. He was kind of assuming she wasn't part of the show, and he hoped she wasn't offended. Just because she was deaf, that didn't mean she couldn't be in theater, right?

But she nodded yes; she was here waiting for someone too. Harlan didn't say anything for a second, and there was kind of an awkward silence—which was funny, because they'd been silent ever since they'd started signing. The theater floor, he noticed, smelled of ammonia and dirt.

He stood up and started to move over a seat. *Come on. We'll wait together.* Harlan wasn't sure why he'd done that. All of a sudden, he just didn't feel like being alone.

It's okay, Elsa signed. *I'll sit over here.* She took a seat on the opposite side of the aisle. Harlan remembered that Deaf people—with a capital "D," since this referred to Deaf culture—generally liked greater personal space so they could Sign more comfortably.

Harlan lowered himself back down and they sat across from each other, watching the actors for a moment. They were walking through a scene with the director, coordinating with whoever was controlling the lights, trying to get the look just right. But they were also joking with one another and laughing. Two guys were having a mock sword fight with plastic swords.

To Harlan's surprise, it looked like fun. He'd only been to a school play once before, to see Amber in *Guys and Dolls,* but he'd spent the whole time in this same back row, snickering with his friends.

You ever do any acting? Elsa said. The light from the lobby made it so they could easily read each other's signing.

I think I've been acting every day of my life, he replied.

Why had he told her that? He didn't even know this girl. It was something about Sign. He could say things without having to actually say them.

You should try out for a play, Elsa signed.

He nodded, but he was thinking, Uh-huh, right. There was no way his mom would stand for him appearing in a play. He heard how she talked about actors, about how flighty they were, how so many were gay. And then, of course, there were his friends; he could just hear what Jerry Blain would say about Harlan in tights.

You have a boyfriend? he signed. *Is that who you're waiting for?* He wasn't sure what made him ask the question. He was just curious.

She shook her head no, but just a touch too emphatically.

What? he asked.

Nothing. She was blushing. It was obvious.

Some guy you wish was your boyfriend?

She shook her head, even more forcefully than

before. Suddenly she wouldn't look him in the eye.

He smirked. *There is!* He was flirting with The Deaf Girl. There was him being charming and there was flirting, and Harlan knew the difference. But why not? The Deaf Girl would be kind of cute when her acne finally cleared up. *Does he know?* he asked.

No! Definitely not.

You might be surprised. Not all guys are as clueless as you think.

He's not clueless, Elsa said. *He just doesn't know.*

Maybe you should tell him.

She leaned back in her chair, splayed out like she'd been stabbed with a knife. *No! I could never!*

Harlan looked back at the stage. They were singing now, to a piano accompaniment—Julian Mercurio as Lancelot singing "If Ever I Would Leave You" to Amber as Guinevere. They looked like they were really in love. Harlan couldn't remember the last time he and Amber had looked like that. Maybe never. Even so, Harlan wasn't jealous. On the contrary, he hoped Julian really felt what he was singing. Then maybe he'd ask Amber out—she might go, even though Julian was in Drama Club—and Harlan wouldn't have to deal with her anymore.

He felt Elsa watching him.

What? he asked.

You want to break up with her, don't you?

What? Her signing had been fast, but the truth was, he'd understood her perfectly.

She looked away. *I'm sorry; never mind. I shouldn't have said that.*

Why did you say it? Harlan signed.

Something about the way you were looking at her.

He was immediately uneasy. Elsa wasn't going to tell, was she? She might not "talk," but she could still get the word out. And it would definitely get back to Amber. Everything did. Amber was a satellite dish for school gossip.

But he couldn't lie to Elsa. Not now. It just felt wrong.

She doesn't understand anything, he said. *I can't believe we're even together.* He hesitated. Should he tell her the rest? *She's not the reason I came into the theater. I'm not waiting for her.*

You're not? Elsa said.

It's complicated. You'll think I'm crazy.

She shook her head—not enough to make it seem like she was dying to hear what he had to say; just enough to make her seem sincere. *I won't,* she said.

My life is all screwed up, he signed. *I don't get to decide anything for myself. I don't have any control.*

Sounds pretty normal to me.

This is exactly what Amber had said; it's what *everybody* said. Everyone seemed to think that his problems were just the same as any other teenager's. But he'd seen his friends' lives up close, and yeah, they all had their shit. But his situation—his *mother*, that is—really *was* worse. Or maybe he was just being arrogant—poor little rich kid? It's not like he was being raised by a crack whore.

But it must be tough, Elsa went on. *Being the son of a senator.*

He looked at her, swallowing her with his eyes. *You have no idea. It didn't used to bother me. But suddenly it does.*

She stared at him too, not taken aback, just curious and genuinely sympathetic. *Why? What's going on now?*

I have these feelings, he said. *That something terrible is going to happen to me, and I have no way to stop it.*

Feelings?

Premonitions. Why had he told her this? Was it still the sign language thing? And what if she told others?

But she wasn't going to tell. Somehow he knew that. His secrets were safe with her.

I need to do something—a specific thing—to keep them from coming true, he went on. *But I don't know what it is.*

You need more control, Elsa said. *Boy, do I get that.*

"What?" Without thinking, Harlan had spoken out loud.

What what?

"What do you mean about control?"

Isn't that what you just said? Elsa said. *That you feel like you don't have any control? I thought that's what you thought was causing the premonitions.*

Harlan kept looking at Elsa. If anyone understood the whole issue of control, it would probably be a deaf person—someone who lost the ability to communicate when the other person's back was turned, and who always depended upon the interpreter's showing up on time. But was Elsa right about him? Was that really what the premonitions were all about?

It sure *felt* right. The two issues were definitely connected: the premonitions made him feel out of control, and his mom didn't let him *have* any control.

He needed to stand up to his mom. What did Harlan have to lose by doing that? If that was the answer, his premonitions might stop for good—and he might also be preventing some very real disaster. And if he was wrong, well at least Harlan would have stood up for himself at last!

What about you? Harlan asked. *Are you going to tell that guy you're hot for him?*

Elsa smiled. *God, no! Besides, we're talking about* your *problems, not mine!*

Harlan smiled too, even as they went on signing. For the first time in a long time, he was actually having fun. It felt like he'd come up for air at last and he could finally really breathe again.

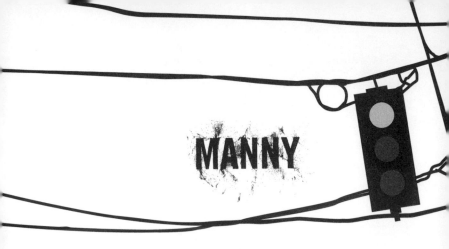

MANNY

The head of a camel. That's what was inside the jack-in-the-box: the grinning head of a silly, big-nosed camel. Manny knew that now, but not because he'd seen the thing again. No, he'd searched all over the house and, sure enough, there'd been no sign of it anywhere.

Finally, Manny had had the bright idea to look it up online. He didn't have much to work with, just his memory of what it looked like on the outside—the colored sides and the carved letters. It had taken a while to track it down, but eventually he'd found it on eBay—a classic Shropshire Sahara jack-in-the-box, made in England in 1912.

The current bid was four hundred and twenty-five dollars.

In other words, it was an *expensive* jack-in-the-box. He wondered if his dad knew that. For that matter, how in the world had he bought it for Manny in the first place? He sure didn't have that kind of money now. Had he been a lot richer when Manny was a kid?

Seeing the inside of the jack-in-the-box, knowing it was a smiling camel's head, hadn't triggered any repressed memories of his childhood. At least the on-screen image hadn't done it. Manny knew he needed to see the actual jack-in-the-box. He needed to hold it in his hands, feel it, turn the crank and watch the camel head pop up out of the box.

He heaved a sigh and pushed himself away from the computer. Manny felt a little like a jack-in-the-box himself: if he didn't get out of his house right then, he was sure he was going to burst right up through the roof.

It wasn't until after he'd bought a burger and onion rings, then taken a seat in the dining area, that it occurred to Manny how ironic it was that he'd chosen this particular restaurant. Out of all the restaurants in the city, even all the different fast food restaurants alone, he had to come and eat at a damn *Jack in the Box*? Apparently his subconscious mind had a sense of humor. Between that and his nightmares, his brain was just a barrel of laughs.

But Manny was starving and he'd already bought his food, so he figured there was no sense in wasting it.

He took a bite from his burger. As he did, he spotted a second reason why coming to this Jack in the Box had been a bad idea. Ricky Loduca, a jock from his school, was over by the order counter. He was carrying a tray heavy with food and scanning the seating area for an empty table.

Manny immediately looked down at his onion rings. This was just what he needed: to be hassled by a jock. It was impossible that Ricky wouldn't see him—the restaurant only had six tables. But maybe he'd pretend like they didn't know each other. For that matter, maybe Ricky really *didn't* know him. After all, Ricky was a star swimmer at a school where the swim team was actually a pretty big deal, and Manny was just a theater geek.

"Hey!" Ricky said, stopping in front of Manny's table, grinning from ear to ear. "I know you!"

Against his will, Manny looked up. "Oh. Hey." *Did* they "know" each other? Yeah, they went to the same school, but they'd never even said three words to each other before.

"All by your lonesome, huh?" Ricky said, and Manny shrugged. "It's Manny, right?"

"Yeah," Manny said, surprised that Ricky knew his name. And that's when Manny remembered something important about Ricky. He was gay. He'd come out the year before, in an article in the school newspaper. Manny wasn't quite as shocked as everyone else; after all, Manny *was* in the theater, so he knew openly gay people. But it wasn't every school where one of the star jocks comes out of the closet, so Manny had still been surprised.

"You alone too?" Manny said.

Ricky nodded. "Yeah."

There was an uncomfortable silence. Awkwardly holding the tray in one hand, Ricky scratched his nose.

"You wanna sit?" Manny said. He didn't want company—he had too much to think about already. But it did seem like Ricky was waiting to be asked.

Sure enough, Ricky said, "Yeah, okay!" Then he took the seat across from Manny. There was no hesitation in Ricky's eyes at all. Looking at his face was like looking right into the sun itself, all bright and warm and open—too bright, if you asked Manny. Still, he had to admire the fact that the guy had come out. Unlike the guys in theater, Ricky had had a hell of a lot more to lose.

"So," Ricky said. "What's goin' on?"

121

Manny took a bite of his burger. "Nothing much."

There was another silence. Manny was already regretting the situation. They were from such different worlds. What would they have to talk about? What if Ricky thought Manny was trying to pick him up? What if Ricky was trying to pick *him* up?

"You're a swimmer, huh?" Manny said. Even across the table, he could smell the chlorine.

Ricky nodded. "You do sports?"

Manny shook his head. He barely knew how to swim. His dad had never been able to afford lessons, or even admission to the pool. "But I did this video about a soccer player once," Manny said. "No matter how hard she tried, she couldn't kick a goal. Even when she got up really close." Hearing himself out loud, Manny was struck by how stupid he sounded.

But Ricky laughed anyway. "You make movies, huh?"

"Yeah. Plus I do web design. And lighting design for the school plays." Why did Manny suddenly feel the need to justify his existence?

Ricky nodded. "That's cool." He ate his French fries five at a time, like a jock would, not like a gay guy. "Funny. We've been at the same schools for years, but I don't think we've ever talked."

Yeah, Manny thought. And now they knew why.

"How are things?" Manny asked.

"Things?"

"You know. At school."

"Oh," Ricky said. "Okay, I guess. I mean, I have friends—more girls than guys, but still. Everyone's cool. But it's hard sometimes. I know people are watching me." Manny hadn't meant the whole gay thing. Or had he?

"How are things with you?" Ricky asked.

Manny crunched down on an onion ring. "Me? Oh, I'm great. Fantastic."

"Yeah? Then how come you're eating dinner by yourself?"

For a second, Manny felt defensive. Then he saw that Ricky's face was just as sunny as ever, that he hadn't meant anything by it. "I don't know," Manny said. "I just needed to get away for a while."

"Parents?"

"Parent. I don't have a mom."

"Yeah? I don't have a mom either. Well, I have one—she's just not around. People always say it must suck, but I've never known any different."

"Yeah," Manny said, nodding. "That's it exactly. How can you compare it to something you've never had?" Could it be that he actually had something in common with Ricky Loduca, Gay Jock, after all?

"What's goin' on?" Ricky asked. "With your dad?"

Manny didn't want to have this conversation. He had things to think about, antique jack-in-the-boxes to figure out. He shook his head. "It's a long, boring story."

"Come on!" Ricky said. "I still got half a thing of French fries left."

Manny had to smile. He had a feeling that Ricky had that effect on a lot of people. Could Ricky be one of those legendary high school students who were rumored to exist, but whom Manny had never actually encountered before: a popular kid who was also genuinely nice?

"He's hiding something," Manny said. He told Ricky about the nightmares, and the way his dad had reacted when Manny had told him about them.

"Dude!" Ricky said. "That heaps!" This was an expression popular lately—short for "heaps of shit," or something like that. Neither Manny nor any of his geek friends had ever used it.

There was another silence, but not as awkward this time. Ricky's French fries were gone, but he didn't seem to be in any hurry to leave.

"What about you?" Manny asked. "How come you're eating dinner all by yourself?"

"Huh? Oh. Well, my best friend, he's been kind of distracted lately."

"That's lousy."

"It's okay," Ricky said. "After last year, I owe him. Mostly, though, it's my dad."

"What about him?"

Ricky wadded the foil wrapper from his hamburger into a ball. "It's stupid."

"Come on!" Manny said. "I told you my long, boring story!" He could hardly believe it. Was he actually joshing around with a jock? And it didn't seem all that strange! In another place and time, Manny could almost imagine being friends with a guy like him.

Ricky smiled. "Okay, okay!" he said. "My dad makes windows. Stained glass, custom-made. It's the family business, and he wants me to take it over. Loduca and Son. But I don't wanna take it over!"

"What do you want to do?" Manny asked.

"Teach, maybe? But I know what I *don't* want, you know? I mean, I've watched my dad work glass my whole life, and it's just not fun. And then there's the whole gay thing. No son of his, and all that crap."

"That heaps," Manny said quietly. So he'd used the expression at last. And the thing was, it didn't feel all that weird.

"Yeah," Ricky said. "Sometimes I wish I wasn't

adopted. I hate that he can tell himself that I'm not 'really' his son—that 'his' son wouldn't be gay. 'Cause I know that's what he thinks." Ricky turned and tossed the crushed foil wrapper at a garbage can on the other side of the room. He made it perfectly—a natural athlete.

"You're adopted?" Manny asked.

"Yeah. You?"

Manny shook his head. But halfway through the shake, he froze.

"What?" Ricky said.

"*Am* I adopted?" Manny said out loud.

"What do you mean? Don't you know?"

"No baby pictures! And no toys, except for that single one!"

Ricky was confused. "What?"

"Don't you see?" Manny said. "Maybe that's what my dad has been trying to hide from me!"

"Really?"

Manny was thinking out loud. "I mean, that's why there wouldn't be a crib or a trike! And that would explain the jack-in-the-box! I mean, there's no way my dad could have afforded that thing!"

"Okay," Ricky said.

Manny stood up. "Look, I've got to go! But it was really nice talking to you!"

Ricky smiled. "Sure. See you at school."

Would Ricky talk to him at school? Probably, Manny had to admit.

"And Manny?" said Ricky.

Manny turned.

"Good luck!"

Manny smiled back. Then he headed for the door. He was going to confront his dad. And this time, he wouldn't take anything for an answer except the truth.

HARLAN

Harlan was certain he was being watched. It was Tuesday of the following week, and he'd just arrived home from swimming and walked into his bedroom. His dad was away in Washington—of course—and his mom wasn't home yet. But he couldn't shake the feeling that there was someone staring at him. It was crazy: the curtains in his room were drawn, and his webcam wasn't turned on.

He sat down at his computer to check his e-mail. There was a message from Ricky about some cool guy he'd had dinner with. Could it be that Ricky had a boyfriend at last—or was at least finally talking about his love life?

Harlan glanced back at his room. Why did it feel like he wasn't alone? Maybe his mom had installed some kind of hidden camera—like when parents hide camcorders inside teddy bears to spy on the baby-sitter.

Now he really was being crazy.

He turned back to stare at his e-mail inbox. There was nothing from Amber, just like there hadn't been anything from Amber in days. Two weeks ago, before the party and the Ouija board, there would have been five e-mails just from one afternoon alone—links and pictures and stupid jokes. His relationship with Amber was over. So why didn't he have the guts to officially break it off?

Harlan shivered. He could *feel* an eye on him! But whose? He was all alone in his bedroom. Or was he? Maybe it wasn't some*one* watching him—maybe it was some*thing*. He turned his chair around to face the empty room.

And that's when he saw it. His mom had left his mail on his bed. The envelope on top was glossy white, with a close-up photo of a large eyeball. The eyeball looked like it was staring right at him.

Harlan *was* being watched—by a piece of mail! He almost laughed out loud.

He rolled his chair closer to the bed and picked up the envelope. It was from the local eye bank—one of the largest in the country. It held an annual fundraiser called the Eye Ball, which was taking place that weekend. One of the highlights was the Retina Raffle, where people bought tickets for a chance to win these really expensive prizes—trips and cars and weekend getaways. Then, at the end of the dance, there was a drawing. The organizers brought out this big clear plastic bin filled with Ping-Pong balls that had been painted to look like eyes. Each eye also had a little number on it.

Ever since Harlan was nine years old, he'd been the one to draw the winning Ping-Pong ball. It had all been his mom's idea, of course. People got such a kick out of seeing the senator's little boy dressed up in his tuxedo. That idea hadn't used to bother Harlan; maybe it had even made him a little proud, knowing that his mom was so pleased with him. And this year, now that he was seventeen, the coordinators had also made him one of the Eye Ball's eight honorary "Cornea Corporals." But they were just throwing him a bone. They really wanted the cute kid in the tux.

He sighed. Yet another charity event. His mom hadn't asked if he wanted to go—not this year, not any year. She'd just signed him up. And now he'd have to be there for hors d'oeuvres, and he'd have to stay for the raffle. It would all take four hours at least—four hours of his precious weekend.

He tore open the envelope.

There was a letter inside that began, "Dear Harlan: I wanted to thank you in advance for joining us yet again at our annual Eye Ball fund-raiser."

Harlan started to crumple up the letter. But then he stopped. He looked at the signature at the bottom. "Sharon L. Blakely," it read, "Special Events Coordinator."

He stared at it for a second, thinking. What would happen if he told them he couldn't do it this year? After all, he had surely already done his part for the charity itself, going to eight Eye Balls in a row. And they had seven other "Cornea Corporals." It's not like anyone would even notice his absence. They could get some other kid to dress up in a tux and draw the winning Ping-Pong ball, or maybe get a girl—strike a blow for equality while they were at it.

Harlan turned toward his phone and punched in the number of Sharon Blakely. It was after hours, so he got her voice mail.

"Mrs. Blakely?" he said when the time came to leave a message. "This is Harlan Chesterton. I'm afraid I've got some bad news. I'm not going to be able to make the Eye Ball this year. Sorry about the late notice."

He couldn't think of anything else to say, so he

hung up the phone and sat there, staring at the receiver.

Had he really just done that? Had he really withdrawn from a function that his mom had committed him to? And had the world really not come to a screeching halt?

He crumpled up the letter and the glossy envelope with the picture of the eyeball on it. Then he tossed them both into the wastebasket, breathing easy again now that the eye of the world had moved off him at last.

Harlan was on fire, which was quite an achievement given that he was underwater at the time. He couldn't remember the last time he'd swum so hard or with such focus. He felt like a dolphin on *Ginkgo biloba*.

All through the first set, he and Ricky had been pushing each other, going back and forth for the lead. But now they were on the last 100 of the set— their last four lengths of the pool. And Harlan was determined to beat Ricky to the end.

Kicking was the key to speed, Harlan knew: the harder you kicked, the faster your arms moved and the quicker you went through the water. So Harlan kicked furiously. But Ricky knew the key to speed too, and he was kicking just as hard. And by the end of the second length, Harlan wasn't getting any edge.

Suddenly Harlan imagined that the black tile stripe along the floor of the pool was alive, that it was some kind of giant leathery alligator gliding behind him in the water. It rose up underneath him, mouth opening, teeth gleaming in the crystal-clear liquid.

Harlan panicked, but it was a good panic. He fought the creature with his stroke, kicking deep and hard, pulling fast and tight. His legs churned, and his arms plowed deep trenches in the pool.

The creature chased him. It was a shadow underneath him, just out of reach, trying to snatch him with its teeth.

Harlan made the next turn and kept kicking, but he wasn't pulling ahead. In fact, inch by inch, Ricky was slowly pulling ahead of *him*! The black alligator was chasing Ricky too.

Harlan hit his last turn right on the mark, then headed for home. It was all coming down to the last length of the pool, just as it so often did. Ricky was half a body-length ahead now, but Harlan was determined to catch him. He held his breath and kicked. He felt like Moses parting the waters of the Roosevelt High School pool. As for the black leathery alligator, he'd left it far behind in his wake.

Ten yards from the end, Harlan passed Ricky. And

he outtouched his friend by at least a yard.

In a second, Ricky was up and gasping for air, but smiling too. "That was excellent, man! *Excellent!* I haven't swum that hard in *months*! What the hell got into you?"

Harlan was panting and grinning. "I don't know, man! It was just *there*, somewhere inside me!" It wasn't just a question of swimming well; Harlan hadn't been this *alive* in months. It was one of those moments that you want to preserve and display under some kind of glass dome, there to examine whenever you want for the rest of your life. And for the record, Harlan knew exactly what had gotten into him: by pulling out of the Eye Ball, he'd stood up to his mom. And now he couldn't remember ever feeling so free.

He turned to the pool, looking out at the lane, ready to continue the workout.

But a voice said, "Harlan? Can I see you a second?"

Harlan looked up. The swim coach.

"Sure," Harlan said. "What's up?"

Coach Cleveland grew orchids. And there was something about the heat and humidity of the pool area that worked wonders for his flowers. As a result, whenever he had a problem plant, he brought it with him to work. His plants must have been doing really badly lately, because the pool office was full of potted orchids now.

"What's up, Coach?" Harlan asked.

"Uh, Harlan," the coach said. "I'm afraid I have some bad news."

He wants me to swim the 500 in the meet with Lincoln, Harlan thought. Harlan hated the 500—five hundred yards was twenty lengths of the pool. But there were only so many guys on the team who could do it even halfway well. And if the team wasn't at least competitive in the distance events, all the points would just go to the other team.

"Coach?"

Coach Cleveland picked up an orchid pot and fiddled with the pink blossom. Every year, some new swimmer teased him about his flowers and the whole team wound up having to listen to an impassioned lecture from the coach about just how fascinating orchids really are. It always shut everyone up, if only because no one wanted to hear the orchid lecture again.

"You have to go," Coach Cleveland said at last.

"Go?" Harlan didn't understand.

"You have to leave the pool area. The locker room. You're off the team."

Now Harlan *really* didn't understand. *"What?"*

"Look, it's not me. It's the principal."

"Wait a minute! What'd I do?" But even as he said this, he knew what this was all about: his mom. He had pulled out of the Eye Ball. And his mom had found out about it and called the school to have him thrown off the swim team. It was her way of getting back at him. He had expected her to be upset, but he at least thought she would talk to him first!

"Harlan—"

"Look," Harlan said, "I know it's my mom, okay? We're just having an argument about something. This is her way of getting back at me. It doesn't mean anything!"

"Fine. But, Harlan, you're still seventeen, and she *is* your mom. If you don't have her permission to be here, you can't be here. There are legal issues."

"But she's not being fair!"

"Then talk to her. The minute you get her permission again, of course you can come back."

"But—"

Coach Cleveland slammed down the potted plant. "There is no 'but,' Harlan! For God's sake, your dad's the damn senator, okay?"

Harlan found his mom in her "Activity Room"—a small sunroom off the back of the house. She had a whole staff of people to do absolutely everything that needed doing around the house—a maid, a gardener, a cook. Everything except the house decor, which she handled herself. And it was here in the Activity Room that she did her work—her way to "unwind." It was here that she created her elaborate flower arrangements, replaced throughout the house every five days like clockwork. And here, of course, was where she turned out the dozen or so tasteful holiday wreaths that festooned their house each Christmas: tightly wound wire rings of carefully positioned cookies or tiny gifts or shellacked sugarplums—anything but actual evergreen boughs, which she deemed too tacky. Today his mom was working on her "mosaic table"—a small end table that she was resurfacing with a pattern of broken porcelain and glass bits.

Harlan stepped into the room. "What did you do?" he said. He wasn't about to greet her, not now, maybe not ever again.

She didn't look up from her work, didn't greet him either. "What do you mean?"

"Mom, please don't play dumb."

Carefully, she pressed a bit of orange glass into white plaster; the pattern reminded Harlan of a spiderweb.

"You're going to the Eye Ball," she said.

"Why?" he said. "Why is it so damn important that I go?"

"It's important because you made a commitment, and I expect you to honor it." Her voice was as calm as an alpine lake, and just as cold.

"No!" Harlan said. "*You* made a commitment!"

"Harlan, being a member of this family means we all have certain responsibilities. We ask a lot of you, yes. But in return, we provide you with advantages that other children can only dream about."

"Oh, I've done *plenty* for this family! So I take one weekend off. What's the big deal?"

Suddenly she grabbed a plate off a nearby work-table and threw it down to the ground—hard. It shattered on the tiled floor. Harlan jumped in surprise.

Then, without batting an eye, his mother reached down to the floor to retrieve a piece of the broken porcelain—for her mosaic table, of course. "This isn't about the Eye Ball," she said, just as calmly as before.

Oh, very good, Harlan thought. She'd probably been planning that thing with the plate all afternoon—the perfect way to knock him off-balance. But he knew what his mom had said was absolutely right: this *wasn't* about the Eye Ball. It wasn't even about his dad's election. It was about control. Her control of him.

"Well," Harlan said. "It's too late now. I already

told Mrs. Blakely." He could hear the nervousness in his own voice, which meant his mom could certainly hear it too. As much as he hated to admit it, that thing with the plate had rattled him.

"It's not too late," his mom said. "I called Sharon back and told her there was a misunderstanding, and that you will definitely be there."

"You *what?*"

She looked up at him at last. "What part of that didn't you understand?"

"You didn't even talk to me first?"

"Why would I talk to you?"

"That's it, mom! Don't you see? That's it *exactly!* Why would you talk to me? Because it's *my* life!"

"Don't raise your voice. Ludmilla might hear." Ludmilla was their Russian maid.

"I don't *care* if Ludmilla hears! I'm not going."

"Fine." She looked down again. "Then you won't be swimming either."

She had him. He knew that immediately. He had no leverage to use against her whatsoever. Why hadn't he seen this before? Of course she would win this argument, because she had a strategy. Why hadn't he thought to have a strategy?

"All right, I'll go," he whispered.

"What?" she said. Of course she'd heard him. She

just needed to humiliate him a little more.

"I said I'll go to the damn Eye Ball!" This time, even Ludmilla had to have heard him—which is what his mother had probably wanted, anyway. No better way to keep the maid in line than to prove you had your teenage son in line too.

Harlan turned to go. He'd just come from the pool, but he'd only just started on his workout, and anyway, he desperately needed to connect with the water again. He couldn't go back to the high school, not yet, not before his mom called the principal, who would, in turn, contact his coach. No, for today, he'd have to go to the pool at the community center.

Behind him he could feel his mom's eyes on him again, watching his every defeated step. But he wasn't about to look back at her.

Another plate crashed on the floor behind him.

And Harlan jumped again in surprise, exactly like his mother knew he would.

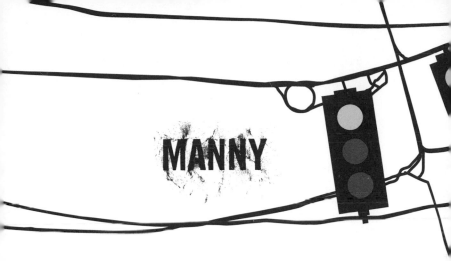

MANNY

Manny couldn't do it; it was impossible. He'd made it all the way to the bottom level of the Chasms of Chaos, and he'd assembled all the pieces of the Key of Life. But he couldn't find Dragonio's Gate anywhere. There was clearly something he was missing, another piece of the puzzle. Was there another, hidden level to the dungeon? A missing piece of key? That was the one thing Manny hated about computer games. For all their talk about "choices" and "interactivity," there was really only one "right" way to win the game. You might have a little latitude about how you got there, but the final outcome was always the same.

Playing this game is stupid, Manny thought. He knew he should be asking his dad about his being adopted. He'd tried to bring it up a couple of times now. But he'd never been able to get the words out.

He wasn't sure why. What was the worst thing that could happen? That he'd learn he was wrong and his dad would be offended by the question?

No. The worst thing that could happen was something he couldn't anticipate, something completely unexpected. If he was right about being adopted, there had to be a reason why his dad had kept the information from him all these years. His subconscious mind seemed to know the reason—and if his nightmares were any indication, it was something serious and scary. So what was the goddamn hurry? Why not wait until the time was exactly right?

Manny saved his game and pushed away from the computer. Everything was all mixed up. He needed to get away, clear his mind, maybe even get some exercise.

He turned to his dresser. The bottom drawer was open, and he spotted a pair of nylon running shorts lying right on top.

"Where are you going?" his dad asked as Manny walked by the kitchen, backpack in tow. The third Tuesday of the month was the night of the partners' dinner down at the law firm, so his dad always got home early. Now he was chopping vegetables on a plastic chopping block.

"Huh?" Manny said. "Oh, the community center. I thought I'd go for a swim."

"What?" his dad asked.

"A swim. Aren't you always saying I need more exercise?"

"But you don't know how to swim."

"I do so know how to swim!" Manny said, offended somehow. "We had to take a week of swimming in P.E."

"You did?"

Manny nodded. "And for the record, I was the only kid in my whole class who had never taken lessons."

"Manny, we couldn't afford it."

"Uh-huh. Funny how we always had money for organic vegetables."

"No," his dad said.

"Huh?"

"You can't go swimming."

"It's okay. I can fake it okay."

"I mean it," his dad said. "You really can't go."

For a second, Manny thought his dad was joking. Then he saw the look on his dad's face. It wasn't disapproval or annoyance. No, there was no expression at all—just as in that earlier dream of Manny's.

What was going on? Did it have something to do with the incident with the jack-in-the-box? But that had been over a week ago, and there hadn't been any weirdness in the air since then.

"Are you serious?" Manny asked.

"There's something I need you to do for me," his dad said.

"Right now?"

"Right now."

"Well, what *is* it?" Manny didn't try to hide his annoyance.

His dad didn't answer, just started hacking at a head of broccoli. Did he have a chore for Manny or not? It almost seemed like he was stalling for time. Finally, his dad glanced out the window, and Manny swore he saw relief flash across his face.

"We have a clog in one of our gutters," his dad said. "It's not draining right. You need to clear it."

"Right this very minute?"

"Manny, do you know how much damage a clogged gutter can do?"

"But—"

"Manny, please. Just do this for me, okay?"

Manny got the ladder from the garage and climbed up to the offending gutter. It was cold outside, but not freezing. Even so, he could see his breath in the wet winter air.

There was water standing in the gutter itself. It hadn't rained in a couple of days, so his dad hadn't been blowing smoke when he'd said the gutter was clogged. The water was brown and stagnant, full of dead leaves that had probably been festering there since fall. Manny hadn't remembered to wear rubber gloves, but he didn't want to climb all the way back down now, so he reached inside and just started rooting about in the mess. It was cold—even colder than he'd expected—and the icy chill actually stung his hand. Stirring up the water released a foul smell. Short of scooping dog poop off the lawn, this was about as unpleasant as yard work got.

Why was Manny doing this? Yeah, sure, because his dad had asked him to. But that wasn't the real reason. The real reason he was on the roof was the same reason he'd been playing that computer game and then heading for the swimming pool. It was all a question of avoidance. And what was Manny avoiding? Saying out loud the words, "Dad, am I adopted?"

Manny had pulled five or six handfuls of rotting leaves from the gutter, but it still wasn't draining. Whatever was clogging it was wedged deep in the downspout itself. He would have to reach down and see what he could find. With a sigh, he pushed up his sleeve and stuck his arm inside. But the added volume caused the water in the gutter to overflow; it spilled onto him, soaking the front of his sweatshirt.

"*Goddamn it!*" Manny said, and the words echoed off the neighbors' garage. He had exclaimed partly in frustration about the cold water and the fact that he'd been wearing a clean sweatshirt. But it was mostly frustration with himself, the way he was being so cowardly with his dad. Did that make Manny a coward? It was true that he'd also never been able to stand up to the jocks at school, but that was more a question of self-preservation.

Manny's fingers brushed something deep inside the downspout. By now he'd lost almost all the feeling in his hand, so it wasn't clear what he was touching. Whatever it was, it had to be what was blocking the flow of water. But for the moment, it was just out of his reach.

He leaned in closer, careful not to lose his balance on the ladder. He only needed another inch or two. Cold water soaked up to the shoulder of his sweatshirt, but he was already so wet that it didn't matter.

Finally he had it. His fingers closed around something pliable, but with a brittle, spiky exterior. A pinecone? He pulled on it, but it was wedged in there pretty tightly.

I'll do it, Manny thought to himself. He'd finish

with the downspout, and then he'd confront his dad. Because no matter what his dad told him, it had to be better than not knowing.

Manny gave the clog a hard jerk, and finally it gave way. He lifted it up through the muck. Still more water splashed out of the gutter, but at least he'd gotten the obstruction. He lifted it up so he could see what it was.

A dead pigeon. It had to have been in there for weeks, and it was partly decomposed. The eye sockets were empty, and the body was soft and bloated. It was the broken feathers and curled claws that had felt prickly in his hand.

"Eewww!" Manny said, flinging the bird away, almost losing his balance.

He started down. First, he was going to go inside and scrub his hand with soap. Then, a promise to himself was a promise. He was going to have it out with his dad.

"Dad?" Manny said back in the kitchen. His father started in surprise. He'd been slicing a cube of tofu. Meanwhile, Manny hadn't even bothered to change out of his wet clothes.

"Manny," his dad said. "What is it? Did you clear the gutter?"

147

"It's taken care of. But now I want to ask you something."

"Did you check the others? Because they might have clogs too."

"Am I adopted?"

On the stove, onions sizzled in a frying pan.

"What?" his dad said.

Manny repeated the question, even though he knew his dad had heard him perfectly.

There was another hesitation. Then his father laughed. "What makes you think that?"

But his dad's hesitation had already answered Manny's question.

"Why didn't you ever tell me?" Manny asked.

His dad stood by the stove a very long time, until the onions started to smoke. Then he turned off the burner and walked to the kitchen table and sat down.

"How did you know?" his dad said.

Manny took the seat across from him. "I'm not sure exactly. It was just a feeling. That something wasn't right."

"There's nothing wrong with being adopted."

"I don't mean with that. I mean with us."

His dad nodded once.

"Why didn't you tell me?" Manny asked. "If you

don't think there's anything wrong with being adopted, why did you keep it a secret?"

His dad searched the Formica tabletop, as if for an answer. "I don't know," he said at last. "You were just such a sensitive baby."

"So?"

"So there's a stigma."

"Not anymore."

"You don't understand," his dad said. "I was a single father."

"What do you mean?" Manny said. "What about Mom?"

His dad thought for a second. "I didn't adopt you until after she died. I guess it was my way of moving on."

Manny thought about all this new information. The man and woman he'd thought were his parents weren't his parents at all—and the woman he'd thought was his mother wasn't even his *adoptive* mother.

"Anyway," his dad went on, "people judge you when you're a single man who adopts. People think you're depriving the child of a mother."

Manny didn't say anything. He couldn't deny what his dad was saying.

"So we moved," his dad said. "We left town, came

to the city. We left everything and everyone behind. Then people wouldn't know I adopted you."

Manny nodded. That explained why they didn't have any old friends, or old basement junk either.

"What do you know about my—" Manny almost said "parents," but he stopped himself in time. His dad *was* his parent. His being adopted didn't change that. "My birth parents?" Manny finished.

"Not much," his dad said. "They were killed in a car accident. You were home with a baby-sitter."

A car accident, Manny thought.

"How old was I?" he asked.

"Almost three. That's what I always wanted to explain to people. Adoptive parents want babies. They'd rather have a baby of a different race or the wrong sex than a toddler of the same race. They want to make their mark. Or maybe they're just afraid that the birth parents have already messed the kid up and it's too late to change him back. Anyway, at three years old, you would've been hard to place, even though you were white. I was doing a good thing!"

"Dad! Of course you were!"

He sighed. "I'm sorry, Manny. I'm sorry I lied to you." Manny was all set to say that he understood, that his dad didn't have anything to be sorry for. But before he had a chance to speak, his dad said,

"But now I've got to get back to my stir-fry. Let's talk about this later, okay? Why don't you go check the rest of those gutters before it gets dark?"

That was it? He was dismissed? Manny wanted to say more, to have his dad say more to him too. He would've thought his dad would have *wanted* to say more; that was the way he usually worked. But apparently there was nothing more *to* say, at least not now. They'd talk about this again later, his dad had said. But would they? It had sounded kind of final to Manny. And now he was just supposed to go outside and check on the gutters?

Manny didn't go back outside. He went up to his room to undress for a shower. As he did, he looked out the window. He could see the gutter from there, the one he thought he'd cleared when he removed the dead bird. It hadn't drained. The gutter was clogged by something deeper still.

HARLAN

Harlan felt like every eye in the room was on him—
which was saying something, since it was the night of
the annual Eye Ball and the whole room was decorated
with eyeballs of every sort. There were thousands of
eyes in all: eyeball balloons, plastic anatomic eye
models for the table centerpieces, even eyeball ice
cubes in the punch.

Of course, the two eyes that mattered most were
his mother's. He could sense them trained on him
like the scope of an assassin. But Harlan wasn't about
to give her the satisfaction of looking back at her, of
acknowledging her existence. He also wasn't going to
talk to anyone. Nope, he was just going to stand
there by the wall, Pepsi in hand, staring listlessly out
at the dance floor. His mom had forced him to come
to this thing, but she couldn't make him mingle—

"shake out some votes," as the Senator liked to say.

His mom wasn't even supposed to be here. This was supposed to be a solo Harlan gig. But she'd made it a point to come tonight because she'd sensed dissension in the ranks. She'd blackmailed him into going and now she *had* to come, to make sure he did what he'd said he would do. But even she couldn't make him do any more than fulfill the letter of the law.

"Harlan!" said a familiar voice. "I've been looking all over for you."

It was Beth Farrell, the novelist he'd met at the Bittle Society dinner. With all the charity and fund-raising events Harlan had attended, he'd never seen her before that dinner; now he'd run into her twice in a matter of weeks. What were the odds?

"Ms. Farrell," he said, nodding politely.

"Beth!" she chastised him.

"Right. Beth. You were looking for me?"

"I was." Suddenly she was digging into her handbag, which was far too large to be in any way fashionable. "I wanted to give you . . ." She kept rummaging until she finally found what she wanted. "This!" And with that, she produced a book. The title was *The Moment of Truth*, and the cover was a picture of a man looking into a mirror, while the face in the mirror was looking away.

Harlan read the name of the author. "It's yours," he said.

"I seem to recall your saying you'd never read me. Here's your chance. Signed by the author and everything."

Harlan smiled. "How'd you know I'd be here tonight?"

"Oh, I read something somewhere about your being a 'Cornea Crony.'"

"'Corporal'!"

"Right!" Beth smirked. "Anyway, I figured anyone who had to put up with an embarrassing name like that deserved at least one freebie."

"Well, thank you," he said, reaching for the book.

She pulled it back from his hand. "But I'm only giving it to you on one condition."

"What's that?"

"If you don't like it, you have to lie and tell me you do."

"You don't have to worry. I'm sure I'll love it."

"Now what did I just say?" Beth said. "You have to lie *convincingly*. There's no way you can know you'll like my book until after you've read it!"

"But I'm not lying. I know I *will* like your book."

She looked at him wryly. "How in the world can you possibly know that?"

He grinned. "Because I know I like you."

She blushed—the desired response. "Why, Harlan. You little flirt."

"I try." Harlan *was* flirting—with a thirty-five-year-old woman, no less. It felt good to feel like his old self again.

He looked over at his mom, on the other side of the dance floor. She was pretending to talk to the wife of the city manager, but she was really watching Harlan. He knew exactly what she thought about his talking to Beth Farrell again. It made him happy to know that he was driving his mom crazy.

Harlan turned back to Beth Farrell. "Can I ask you a question?"

"Anything. I'm an open—well, you know."

"Is it weird to have fans? People who feel like they know you because of your books?"

"Oh, you have *no* idea," Beth said. "It's very flattering, of course. But mostly, I just keep wondering when they're all going to realize what a fraud I am." She grimaced. "I guess you could say I'm not very comfortable being in the spotlight."

Harlan nodded. "Uh-huh."

"Oh, please!" Beth said. "Don't pretend you can relate, because I know you can't. You were born to be the center of attention."

"Well, I guess I am kind of a people person," Harlan admitted.

Beth laughed. "I'll say you are." She thought for a second, then said, "I once read this great definition of the difference between an introvert and an extrovert. An introvert is someone who gets energy from being alone, and who is drained of energy by being around other people. An extrovert is the exact opposite—someone who gets energy from other people, and who is drained by being alone."

Harlan nodded. "Everything being equal, I guess I'd rather be around people." *Certain* people, anyway, he thought.

"Ever do any acting?" Beth said. "Spending time in an actual spotlight?"

"Harlan," said the voice of Harlan's mom. "I need to speak to you a moment."

His mom? Where had she come from? He'd been so busy talking to Beth that he'd lost sight of her.

"Excuse us, won't you?" his mom said to Beth, in a voice so innocent that it made Harlan want to strangle her. He felt like he should say something—object to his mom's interruption of their conversation. So why didn't he?

Beth gave his mom a look that was equal parts amusement and disgust. Then she turned to Harlan.

"Be sure and tell me what you think of my book," she said. "But remember: I want praise, not the truth."

And then she was gone, and Harlan was alone with his mom. He was furious with her, but didn't know where to begin. But before he *could* begin, she grabbed Beth's book from his hand. "I'll take that," she said.

Harlan found his voice at last. "Mom! You can't just interrupt me like that! And that's *my* book!" Could she *be* more of a bitch!

"I was just going to hold it for you," she said, even more innocently than before, in a tone so convincing that it almost had Harlan fooled.

"Hold it? Why?"

"Because you're on. You've got to go up now and pick the winning raffle numbers."

Harlan stood behind the stage—really just a raised wooden platform underneath hanging lights. He was waiting for Dr. James Berman, the evening's "'Macula' of Ceremonies," to finish describing all the prizes in the Retina Raffle. In just a moment, he'd introduce Harlan so he could go up onto the stage to pick the winning numbers.

But that was one stage Harlan didn't want to be on. It wasn't that he was afraid of the spotlight or the crowd—he'd told Beth the truth when he'd said he was comfortable being in front of people. What he didn't like was being there on orders from his mom. But he *did* have to go up onto that stage; he didn't have a choice, not if he wanted to keep swimming.

"Third prize is for all you husbands whose wives say you never do anything romantic," Dr. Berman was saying into the microphone. "It's the perfect night on the town, starting with dinner for two at the Rose and Lobster!"

Out on the dance floor and at the surrounding tables, people applauded. Dr. Berman went on explaining the details of the prize. But Harlan shivered. The hall wasn't cold—on the contrary, people had been dancing, and the air was stuffy. But he felt a strange chill.

"Our second prize will be a real treat for the shopaholics in our audience," Dr. Berman was saying. "The merchants at North Park Mall have all gotten together to donate a five-hundred-dollar gift certificate!"

An image flickered in Harlan's mind—but it was vague, too dark to make out. Was he having one of his premonitions? Here? Now? In front of all these people?

No, he thought. He had to fight it—to use that

anti-premonition technique he'd used before. He deliberately slowed his breathing and imagined himself on life support, trying to make the filling and emptying of his lungs as even as possible. Then he forced himself to concentrate on the here and now, to be aware of every little thing going on around him.

"And for the grand prize in the Retina Raffle," Dr. Berman was saying, "a week-long trip for two to Hawaii!"

Harlan's technique wasn't working; no matter how hard he tried, he didn't seem to be able to stop this premonition from coming. But this one was different from all the others. The feeling of dread was getting stronger and stronger and the image in his mind was somehow growing bigger, but it still wasn't any clearer; it was just a haze, completely indistinct. And yet the uncertainty of this vision, its elusiveness, actually made it even more unsettling than any of his other premonitions.

"Harlan?" whispered a voice. "That's your cue."

Harlan turned. Sharon Blakely, the special events coordinator, was standing beside him. She was staring out at the stage, toward Dr. Berman and the audience beyond.

"Huh?" Harlan said.

She smiled at him reassuringly. "You're on." Sure

enough, Harlan heard applause coming from the hall. But Harlan didn't—couldn't!—move. Sweat dripped from his scalp. It felt like he was breathing through a pillow.

"Harlan?" Sharon said. "Are you okay?"

He wasn't okay. By now, the vision had expanded to fill his brain, but it still wasn't focused. It was infuriating, like the blind spot in the corner of your eye that, when you look right at it, isn't there anymore.

Out in the audience, the applause faded away—abruptly, impatiently, almost like someone had pulled a plug.

"Harlan?" Dr. Berman said, up onstage, in a mock sing-song voice. "We're waiting!"

"Harlan!" said Sharon, beside him, more emphatically.

But suddenly he felt a new presence near him behind that stage.

"Harlan?" his mom said. "What are you doing? Why aren't you going on?"

He looked at her, but he couldn't get enough of a breath to speak. It was like she was one of those vacuum pumps that are used to preserve food and she had sucked what was left of his air right out him.

He shook his head no.

"Don't be ridiculous," she said. "I don't know

what you're trying to pull here, but it's not going to work. Now get up there."

She pushed him up the small set of steps.

Harlan stood at the top of those stairs, in the shadows at the back of the platform, out of the range of the hanging stage lights overhead. He felt like a quadriplegic—someone with no control over his arms or legs. But quadriplegics could at least blink; Harlan couldn't even do that. It was all he could do to keep from collapsing into a puddle of saline solution.

His mom had followed him up the steps. She pushed him again, and momentum alone sent him stumbling forward, through a curtain of light and into the glow of the brightly lit stage.

"Ah!" Dr. Berman said to Harlan. "I see you decided to join us at last."

But it was at that exact moment that the premonition crystallized in his mind. It was an image of . . .

Nothing. Harlan had never seen, or even imagined, anything like it. It wasn't darkness or gloom or haze or shadows or fog. It was *nothing*. A void, a vacuum—the absence of matter, of light, of *anything*!

As if Harlan himself did not exist.

It was true that all of Harlan's premonitions so far

had involved the prospect of his own death. But this one went even further, *beyond* death, to the nonexistence—the terrible nothingness—that came after. Or was this just a glimpse of what it meant to have no self?

The "image" tore through his brain like a chain saw. He did not *exist*! Suddenly, the mind's eye was a hollow socket and his soul was a bottomless pit.

Harlan was overwhelmed by what he saw—or, rather, the infinite emptiness that he felt.

Dr. Berman saw the panic on Harlan's face. "All right, then," he said, taken aback. "Let's just get to it, shall we?" And then he turned to the bin with all the numbered Ping-Pong balls.

Harlan swayed awkwardly. Sirens rang in his head; every mitochondrion in every cell of his body called out in alarm. He glanced back behind the stage and saw his mother gesticulating at him like an outraged mime.

"Harlan?" Dr. Berman said, looking around for the cute boy in the tux. Finally he found him, still at the back of the stage. "Oh. There you still are." He made an exaggerated motion with his arm. "Well, get out here! Trying to generate a little suspense, eh?"

Out in the audience, people chuckled. They knew the senator's son, and they knew how out of character this was. So they assumed this had to be some kind of gag—a skit of some sort.

"Look," Dr. Berman said, "I can't move this bin. You have to come to me."

The audience roared.

Harlan stumbled a little, but caught himself and somehow kept himself standing upright. The audience mistook his motion for a step and applauded encouragingly.

"That's it!" Dr. Berman said. "There we go."

"*Go!*" his mom whispered.

And then the void in Harlan's mind began to suck him in. It was slow at first, just a gentle tug on the edges of his being. But it was already picking up pressure, like the intake of a jet engine as it revved up for takeoff.

Harlan could not stay. If he didn't leave that stage then and there, he knew he would simply cease to exist. His soul would be sucked away like so much loose lint.

He turned to go. It was the easiest, most satisfying step of his entire life. He felt like Johnny Appleseed taking his first step on the American frontier, or Niels Bohr walking into his first physics lab. Harlan was *born* to walk off that stage.

Better still, the horrible nothing in his mind was instantly gone.

He thudded down the stairs, past his mother.

"*Harlan!*" she said. "What are you *doing?*"

It didn't matter. She could put shackles on his legs to keep him from swimming, or banish him to some forsaken dungeon. He wasn't going back onto that stage.

"Harlan!" she hissed. "Don't you do this! Don't you *dare*—"

Harlan ignored her, just turned and hurried straight for the nearest exit.

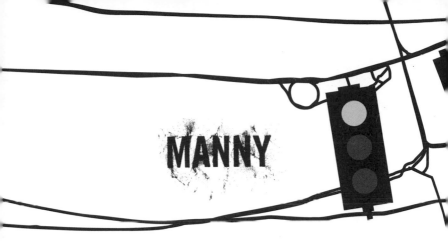

MANNY

There was no exit.

Manny stared at the mess in front of him. The ceiling had collapsed, trapping him inside the cave. It was a wonder he had survived at all.

He adjusted the light on top of his miner's helmet. Dust swirled in the beam like so many miniature galaxies. The falling of the ceiling had changed everything. The wall where he had been excavating had been ripped open. While digging, he had been certain that there was a vein of gold just behind that wall, but he saw now that there wasn't. Just more rock.

Even worse, his exit was blocked. What had once been an opening was now a wall of boulders. He could never dig his way through, especially since all he had was a plastic miner's pick—a child's toy.

On the ground directly in front of him was a pair of crushed wire-rim glasses. All that remained of a fellow miner killed by the collapse? Manny didn't remember having a co-worker; he thought he'd been alone in this cave.

What was he going to do? This was a mine shaft, not a natural cave, and there was only one exit. Now it was blocked, and he was trapped. Soon he would run out of air and die.

He looked again at the swirling motes of dust in the beam of his helmet light. They didn't seem to be settling, even though the collapse was long since over. On the contrary, they whirled and spun about him faster than ever. It was almost as if Manny felt a *breeze* in the air. Could it be there was another exit?

He aimed his light up at the ceiling and, sure enough, spotted a jagged opening in the rock. The collapse had sealed the entrance to the cave, but it had also opened a breach.

He crawled up the mound of boulders, toward the opening in the ceiling. Would it be wide enough to crawl through?

Yes! He reached the opening and saw that it would be a tight fit, but that he could just squeeze through.

Manny clawed his way inside, into a chasm that

led straight upward. The two sides to the rift were close enough together that he would be able to support himself on either side and climb up it like a chimney. Already he could see the top—and daylight! He could even see clouds.

He started edging his way up the chasm, determined to reach the top. From above, he heard a distant roar, like a waterfall. For a second, he thought he smelled gasoline—or was it just the odor of some seeping subterranean gas?

Finally his fingers gripped the edge at the top of the chasm. With a grunt, he pulled himself out of the gash in the ground.

Freedom! he thought as he fought his way up into the open air. The land around him was flat—concrete, a parking lot perhaps. Even as he struggled to make sense of the sight, he registered the sound of something squealing behind him.

He turned. And that's when Manny realized he had crawled up onto a freeway—and right into the face of oncoming truck.

Adopted! Elsa signed. *I can't believe you're adopted and your dad never told you!*

I know, Manny said. *Some big news, huh?*

It was afternoon, and he and Elsa had walked to a

park near school. He'd waited all day for a time and place where there weren't other people around, so he could tell her what he'd learned.

So that's what he's been hiding? Elsa signed.

Manny nodded. *I guess so.*

This park was known for its outdoor displays of petrified wood. There had always been a lot of fossilized wood in the area, and years ago, during the Great Depression, work crews had been hired to take the rocks and arrange them into various shapes, using mortar to seal them in place. But the crews had been laborers, not artists, and their work was mostly of the pyramid-and-snowman sort. The result had to be one of the weirdest parks Manny would ever see.

As they walked amid the stone sculptures, Manny felt Elsa staring at him. *Are you okay?* she signed.

What do you mean? Manny asked.

Well, it must be a big shock.

What? That I'm adopted?

Elsa nodded.

It's not that big a deal, Manny signed. *A lot of people are adopted.*

Yeah, but their dads didn't lie about it.

They stopped in front of what appeared to be a sculpture of a cannon. The petrified wood was mostly pink and blue. Manny just stared.

Elsa tapped him on the arm. *Manny? What's wrong?*

I had another nightmare last night, Manny said.

That's too bad. What was this one about?

He shook his head. *You don't understand. It's not the nightmare itself. It's the fact that I had it at all. I was certain the nightmares had something to do with the secret my dad was keeping. And that once I figured it out, they'd stop. But I know the secret now, and they still haven't stopped!*

Maybe it was just a coincidence, Elsa said. *Maybe it didn't have anything to do with anything.*

Manny shook his head again. Then he told her about his dream, about the collapse in the ceiling that had changed everything in the cave where he'd been working—how even as it had closed off one exit, it had opened another up. *But it ended in the same goddamn place!* he said. *It ended like all the other nightmares—with me being smashed by something! What does my being crushed have to do with my being adopted, anyway? No, there's something I'm missing.*

Missing? Elsa asked.

About the nightmares!

Elsa watched him for a second. Manny hated it when she did that. It wasn't just that she could read lips; sometimes it seemed like she could read minds too.

Manny, Elsa said at last. *You've been under a lot of stress lately.*

It's my dad! Manny said suddenly. *He's still not telling me the truth!*

Wait a minute, Elsa signed. *Let's just think about this, okay?*

Before he could stop himself, Manny signed, *Goddamn it, Elsa, whose side are you on?*

He immediately regretted the outburst. *Elsa, I'm sorry*, he signed quickly. *I'm really sorry!* He'd never fought with Elsa before; now he'd yelled at her twice in a matter of weeks. All over these stupid nightmares.

Absolutely motionless, she looked at him. It was like she had become an assortment of petrified-wood pieces herself. Manny even imagined he could see the crude lattice of mortar that was holding her together and upright—mortar that was cracked and crumbling. Manny could see something else as well. Not just the hurt in her eyes, though he saw that too. Suddenly, even though he didn't want to, it was like Manny could read *her* mind.

Elsa was in love with him. He didn't understand how he'd never seen this before. It was so obvious in retrospect—the way she doted on him, was always so cheerful around him. Manny knew other deaf people,

Elsa's friends, but none of them watched him the way she did, read every word he spoke. Then again, maybe Manny *had* seen the way Elsa felt about him, or at least glimpses of it, but he'd turned away, not wanting to accept the truth. Even now, he had a hard time imagining that anyone could ever truly be in love with a backstage geek like him. But in any event, he also knew, just as clearly, that he didn't feel the same way about her. Manny couldn't explain why; he certainly "loved" her. Just not like she loved him.

Elsa, say something, Manny signed. *Tell me you're okay.*

She smiled. *Of course I'm okay! And all the proof* Manny needed of her love for him was right there in her quick and easy forgiveness.

You told me you wondered why your dad didn't have any baby pictures of you, Elsa soldiered on. *Well, this explains it.*

What? he said, shifting gears again. *Oh. Yeah. I was three when my dad adopted me.*

Well, at least he didn't have to change any diapers.

What? Manny was momentarily confused.

I said, at least he didn't have to change any diapers.

That's right, he said, thinking. *He didn't have to change any diapers!*

Elsa was looking at him funny.

171

Something just occurred to me! Manny explained, excited again. *Something my dad said: that I was a sensitive baby. That that's why he didn't tell me about the adoption.*

So?

So how would he know I was a sensitive baby? He didn't adopt me until I was three! Three years old isn't a baby! Now that Manny thought about it, he specifically remembered his dad referring to the boy he'd adopted as a toddler—definitely *not* a baby!

Manny? What are you saying?

He looked across the park, to a small castle made of petrified wood, complete with battlements and arrow slits; he remembered storming it as a kid. *I'm saying my dad is still lying to me.*

There's got to be some kind of explanation.

I'm sure there is, Manny signed. *And I'm going to find out exactly what it is.*

"Dad," Manny said. "We need to talk." It was later that night, and Manny had found him in the family room, watching TV and ironing clothes. The air smelled of steam from the iron. On television was one of those courtroom drama shows.

"Manny," his dad said. "You're home. Damn it, this shirt is missing a button."

"Did you hear me, Dad?" Manny said. "I want to talk to you."

"My sewing kit. Manny, have you seen my sewing kit?"

"Dad, I want you to tell me the truth."

His dad looked at him as if he'd suddenly materialized out of thin air. "About what?"

"You know what! About my past."

"Manny, didn't we just have this conversation?"

"Yes, but you didn't tell me the truth. I'm not adopted, am I? Of course not! Look at us—you and I look almost exactly alike!"

"Manny, you're adopted! I said so, didn't I? Now help me think where I put my sewing kit." One hand on his hip, one on his head, his dad stared around the family room. On television, two good-looking detectives were examining a corpse in the morgue.

"Forget the sewing kit!" Manny said. "I want you to tell me the truth!"

"I did tell you the truth," his dad said. "There's nothing more to tell."

"There *is*! I know there is." Manny told his dad how he'd referred to him as a "baby" even though he'd also said he had adopted him when he was three years old.

His dad laughed. "Manny, is that what this is all

about? I used the wrong word! You were a sensitive *toddler*. Hey, I'm a guy. So I don't use the right baby words!"

Manny shook his head. "That's not it. That's a lie."

"Manny, don't call me a liar!"

"Tell me the truth, Dad." He wasn't angry. It wasn't about that emotion anymore. Now it was about determination.

"Manny, I don't have time for this. I need to find my sewing kit." It wasn't about anger for his dad either—at least not yet.

"Are you my biological father?"

"My bedroom," his dad said. "I think it's under my bed." He started to leave.

But Manny stepped in front of him, blocking his exit. "Dad, I want the truth."

"Manny . . ." He moved to one side, but Manny followed him.

"I mean it, Dad."

"Manny, get out of my way!" So now it *was* about anger for his dad. In a way, Manny was relieved. It proved he was right about his dad hiding something. But the prospect of what his dad had to say scared him too—so much so that he had to fight to keep from shaking.

"Tell me the truth, Dad."

"Manny!"

"Tell me the truth."

"Fine!" he shouted. "I'll tell you the damn *truth*!"

Manny stared at his father, his dad's face collapsing right in front of him. There was only one way out of that cave-in too, and his dad had to know it. But Manny had learned in his nightmare that just because something was an exit didn't mean it led anywhere he particularly wanted to go.

"You *are* adopted," his dad whispered. "But I'm your father too."

"I want to hear it all," Manny said, wary, yet still resolute. "Everything."

His dad couldn't look at him, tried to turn away, but Manny could already see the tears streaming down his cheeks.

But he nodded at last. "Everything," his dad whispered. "This time, I finally will tell it all."

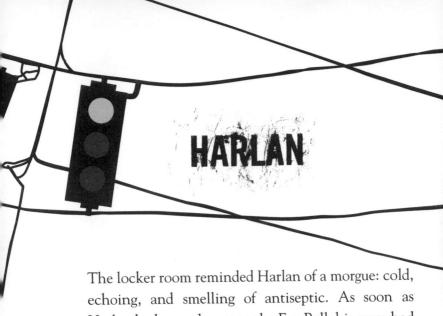

HARLAN

The locker room reminded Harlan of a morgue: cold, echoing, and smelling of antiseptic. As soon as Harlan had agreed to go to the Eye Ball, his mom had called the principal, and he was now back on the swim team. But for the first time in his life, Harlan was in the pool locker room after school and feeling something other than affection.

He found Ricky at his locker, just starting to get undressed.

"Hey," Harlan said. "Can we cut swimming today? I need to talk to you."

Ricky didn't hesitate, just stuffed his things back into his bag and closed his locker. "Sure, man. Let's do it."

They headed out to the football field. They climbed to the top of the wooden bleachers and looked out over the grass, the field's chalk lines blurred by winter neglect. The sun was bright, almost blinding, but the air was cold.

"So," Ricky said. " 'S'up?" Neither had spoken a word since being inside the locker room.

"It's about the way I've been acting lately," Harlan said.

Ricky didn't say anything, just listened.

"This thing happened at the Eye Ball on Saturday," Harlan went on. "I couldn't go onstage." He hesitated a second, not sure how the rest would sound out loud. "I knew something bad was going to happen."

Ricky hesitated too, trying to understand what Harlan was saying. "What do you mean?"

Harlan told Ricky about his premonitions—about how he "saw" horrible disasters in his future. And that while using the Ouija board that night at Jerry Blain's, he'd "seen" himself drowning in the pool at Harriet Tubman.

"So *that's* what was going on that night!" Ricky said. "And why you skipped the meet!"

"I had another premonition earlier, during swim workout. I saw myself being hit by a car. It was so bad I almost drowned."

Ricky nodded. "I remember that too."

"That one came true. A few days later, I was almost hit by a bus. Just like how I'd seen it."

"No shit?"

Harlan looked over at his friend. "No shit. These premonitions, they're *true*. But the one I had onstage at the Eye Ball was the worst of all."

"What was it of?"

Harlan couldn't bring himself to describe out loud what he'd seen—the sense of nothingness. "It was just really bad, okay?"

"Okay," Ricky said.

Harlan stared down into the field of grass. "I want you to tell me the truth. You think I'm crazy?"

"Well, yeah," Ricky said without missing a beat, "but not for having premonitions."

Harlan didn't want to smile, but he did anyway.

"You're not crazy," Ricky said. He said it casually, like it was unbelievably obvious, not like he was trying to get Harlan to believe something he didn't really believe himself.

"But the premonitions!"

"Maybe they're real, maybe not. But one thing is sure: your gut is telling you something. I say listen to it. People lie, even to themselves. But the gut don't lie."

Harlan knew Ricky was talking about his being

gay. But the fact was, Ricky did understand. And he was exactly right. Except he wasn't. Harlan *couldn't* listen to his gut, at least not about standing up to his mother. Not if he wanted to keep swimming.

Harlan kicked paint off the bleacher with the heel of his shoe.

"What?" Ricky said.

"I can't," Harlan said.

"Can't what?"

"Listen to my gut." He sighed. "It's telling me to stand up to my mom."

"So?"

Harlan explained how the one time he had stood up to her, she went and got him kicked off the swim team. "So you see? I can't do it."

"Bullshit!" Ricky said. "Har, are you listening to yourself? You just got through telling me that if you don't listen to your gut, some disaster is going to happen. A *disaster*! You might even die! If your gut is saying the only way to avoid that is to stand up to your mom, you need to listen, dude, *listen*."

"But I also need to swim!" Harlan said.

Ricky shook his head. "No. Swimming's not the same thing. It's great and everything. But swimming's just something you do. It's not who you *are*."

"So what now? What do I do next?"

Ricky thought for a second. Then he said, "You really feel like if you don't stand up to your mom, something bad is gonna happen?"

Harlan sighed again. "I'm sure of it."

Ricky shrugged. "Then you don't have any choice. You have to tell your mom to go to hell."

Harlan found his mother in her dressing room just off the master bedroom. She had a whole network of rooms back there: the dressing room, a walk-in closet, even her own private bathroom, which his dad was not allowed to use. But there were no windows here, making it feel a little like a cave. That seemed fitting, somehow—like Harlan was Beowulf finally confronting Grendel's mother in the depths of her lair.

His mom was sitting at her dressing table, wearing a bathrobe. There was a huge mirror in front of her, but Harlan was standing at the wrong angle, so he couldn't see her face.

"Mom," he said. "There's something I need to say."

She didn't even look over at him. "Not now, Harlan. I have an important dinner tonight, and I need to get ready." Incredibly, Harlan's mom still hadn't said one word to him about his having a panic attack the night of the Eye Ball. Apparently, she couldn't conceive of a son of hers doing such a thing, so it was like she had just decided to pretend it had never happened.

"Yes, now," Harlan said. "It can't wait."

His mom turned to him at last. She hadn't put her face on yet. For the first time since he could remember, he was seeing her without any makeup. She looked drab and gray, like a burned-out lightbulb. But more than anything, she looked sad.

"What is it?" she said. "But make it quick."

"Something needs to change," he said.

"What? What are you talking about?" Did she really not have any idea where this was going? She sure sounded convincing.

But Harlan wasn't giving up that easily. "You can't just tell me what to do anymore."

She turned back to the mirror and picked up a pair of tweezers. As far as she was concerned, this conversation was over.

"Did you hear me?" Harlan said.

She rolled her eyes—or was it just that she was tweezing her eyebrows? "Harlan, I've got a million things to do. There's a new tie on your bed. I'd like you to wear it to the Harris Foundation dinner this weekend, with your navy jacket."

"Mom," he said evenly, "that's exactly what I

mean. I never said I'd go to the Harris Foundation dinner. You never asked. In the future, I'll do two events a month for you and dad. But they'll have to fit into *my* schedule. I think that's fair. And I've already done two events this month, so I won't be going anywhere this weekend."

His mother put down the eyebrow tweezers. "Harlan, didn't we go through this already? Do you *want* to lose your swimming privileges?"

"I don't care about swimming. This is more important than swimming."

"Fine," his mother said. She picked up a bottle of liquid foundation and started smearing it over her face. It made things smooth and uniform, but hard, like porcelain.

He studied the back of her swanlike neck. "Fine, what?" he asked.

"Fine, you won't be swimming anymore. And I wouldn't get too comfortable with that car of yours either."

"Mom," Harlan said, oh-so-patiently, "you saw what happened at the Eye Ball. Did you think I was putting on an act? Don't you see? I can't do it anymore."

She didn't respond. She was determined to keep pretending that the incident at the Eye Ball had never happened.

"Did you hear me?" Harlan said.

"I heard," she answered. "It doesn't change anything."

"Mom, why are you doing this?"

"Doing what? What am I doing?" It sounded like she honestly didn't know.

"Just answer me one question," Harlan said. "Why are you so angry with me?"

She kept working on her face. She put down the bottle of foundation, then picked up another container and started powdering. "Angry at you?" she said. "Do I look like I'm angry at you?"

Yes, Harlan thought, watching her work. She looked absolutely furious. Who else would answer the question "Why are you so angry at me?" with such indifference?

But Harlan didn't budge. "I'm not going to the dinner," he said. "And, for the record, in the future I'll decide my extracurricular activities."

She sighed. "Harlan, I'm sorry you feel that this family is such a terrible burden on you."

"Guilt won't work, Mom. Not this time."

"You're going to the dinner, and that's final. I don't want to talk about it anymore."

"I'm not going, Mom. Get me kicked off the swim team, take my car, I'm still not going."

She just kept working on her face.

"Mom?"

When she still didn't answer, he stepped toward her. She was sitting in a swivel chair, and he reached for her shoulder, to turn her around and make her face him. "Mom, listen—"

The second he touched her, she pulled back, as if recoiling from the brush of a ghost. "Don't touch me."

He withdrew his hand, but he didn't step away. She immediately started working on her face again, but too broadly, awkwardly. She was trying hard not to let Harlan see her sweat, but it wasn't working. So close to her, he could even see her tremble.

"You know what?" Harlan said. "When I came here tonight, I thought this was about the Eye Ball and the Harris Foundation dinner—about the fact that you're threatened by my standing up to you. But now I see that this isn't about that at all. It's about the fact that you've resented me all along. The thing I still don't understand is why. What did I do that makes you so unhappy?"

She froze, eyeliner in hand. "Do you really want to know?"

It took Harlan aback, hearing his mother basically agree that she "resented" him. At the same time, he knew she was only trying to throw him off-balance—like the way she'd smashed the plates on the floor when she was resurfacing that mosaic table.

"I said I did," Harlan said. "And I do."

She swiveled around to face him. He couldn't remember the last time they had been so close—and face-to-face, no less. "You may not like it," she said.

"Tell me," Harlan whispered, unnerved in spite of himself.

"You're adopted," she said matter-of-factly.

Harlan had expected her to say a lot of things. But he hadn't expected this. "What?"

"It's true. You're the son of my brother and his girlfriend."

It's a lie, Harlan thought—another way to throw him off guard. Or was it? Somehow it had the ring of truth.

"I remember the first night you came to us," his mother went on, almost wistfully, as her eyes lost their focus. "Just a baby. You looked so helpless. You reached up to me, desperate to be held. But you barely cried. You had already learned that it didn't make any difference."

"But why— " Harlan started to say.

"Because he was a drunk!" his mother said. All of a sudden, her eyes had their focus back, and more.

185

"Among other things. One night, he got drunk and left you alone in the bathtub. You almost drowned."

H_2O *danger Tub!* The words of the Ouija board hit Harlan right in the gut. That hadn't been a reference to Harriet Tubman High School, or anything in his future; it had been a reference to his *past*, to danger in an actual *tub*—a bathtub he'd been left alone in as a baby! Did this also explain the premonition he'd had that night—of his drowning at what he'd thought was the meet with Harriet Tubman High School? Like all his premonitions, it had been shadowy and unclear. So maybe it wasn't the future he'd seen, but the past; Marilyn Swan had said that the future and the past were often hard to distinguish. Maybe *all* his "premonitions" were impressions from the past! And speaking of Mrs. Swan, this could definitely be what she had meant about an "accident in the water."

But his mom had no way of knowing what Mrs. Swan had told him, or what the spirits—or his own subconscious—had been trying to tell him with the Ouija board. Which meant his mom had to be telling the truth!

It was too much information. Harlan could barely take it all in. But he'd said he wanted the truth, so now he was determined to see it through.

"What happened to them—my parents?" Harlan asked. "Are they still alive?"

"Not your father," his mom said. "Four years after he lost custody to us, he committed suicide."

"Why didn't you tell—" But even as he was speaking, Harlan had another thought: *this* was why his mother resented him! She was finally really telling the truth. Her feelings for Harlan weren't about him at all. They were about her brother—a drunk, "among other things." For the control freak that was his mother, that would have been inexcusable. Had his mom tried to control her brother too, only to lose him in the end? No doubt Harlan looked just like him. (This also explained her obsession with keeping him away from drugs and alcohol; it *wasn't* just about him not embarrassing her and his father.)

"He was crazy, Harlan," his mom said. "Eventually, he even started seeing things."

Seeing things? Harlan thought. As in "premonitions"?

"When I look at you," his mom went on, "at how erratically you've been acting, I see the same thing happening all over again. That's why it's so important that you listen to me, and do the things I ask. If you keep going down the road you're on, you're headed straight for disaster."

Disaster. There was that word again. Was she right? Were his premonitions a sign that he was just like his father—that he was crazy?

Suddenly Harlan started laughing. And all the anxiety and confusion he'd been experiencing? It was gone, like black smoke swept away by a clarifying wind.

His mom pulled her robe tight. "You think this is funny?" she said.

"Yeah," he said. "I think it's hilarious!"

His mom wasn't right; Ricky was. Harlan had to listen to his gut. It was all he had to go on. And even now, his gut was telling him that his mom was full of crap. Oh, her argument that his standing up to her put him on the road to disaster was interesting. There was a reason why his dad's campaign manager and political strategists all ultimately answered to her; she was an expert tactician, and quick on her feet to boot.

But his mom was absolutely wrong when it came to Harlan. As a result, she had to be stopped once and for all. And Harlan had come prepared, with just the right weapon. This time he *did* have a strategy.

Harlan kept laughing, but he wasn't feeling happy so much as serene. So *this* is what wisdom felt like! He'd never experienced anything quite like it before.

"Don't you laugh at me!" his mom said. "And don't you *dare* laugh while—"

"Listen," he said, stopping her in mid-sentence; he didn't think he'd ever stopped her in mid-sentence before. "Things *are* going to be different around here from now on."

"I refuse to listen—"

"Do you know why?"

He'd stopped her again. She didn't answer his question. She looked confused, by throwing the adoption in Harlan's face, she thought she'd won. Now she didn't know how to respond. Her big guns hadn't been so big after all.

Harlan reached into his pocket and pulled out a plastic bag full of white pills.

"Do you know what these are?" he said.

She still didn't speak. Could it be that she was finally at a loss for words? His mom, the woman who wrote the speeches that got his dad elected to the U.S. Senate and who, even now, edited the words churned out by his staff of highly paid speechwriters?

"They're drugs, Mom. Ecstasy, to be exact." He wasn't lying. Jerry Blain was good for something after all.

"What are you—"

"Nothing at all. I'm certainly not taking them, if

189

that's what you're thinking. But here's the deal. Unless you back off, I'll be caught with them."

"You would do that to your—"

"I'd do much more than that," he said, still speaking calmly, evenly. "And think about it. The Senator's son? Caught with Ecstasy? Does Mr. Family Values really want to have to explain that to his fans at the Christian Coalition? Remember how much embarrassment the Bush girls caused their parents?"

Harlan's mom glared at him. What little color there had been in her unrouged cheeks was gone now. It was blackmail, plain and simple: that's what he was doing to her. Just because his mom didn't want him ending up an addict like his biological father, that didn't mean she wasn't aware of the political ramifications too. He hated that he had to resort to such a thing—to lower himself to her level. But he *had* to do it. It was the only way. Sometimes you had to fight fire with fire. Sometimes the path to peace *was* war.

He had her now, and she knew it. He could see it in the set of her jaw. It was over, and he'd won. She was vanquished. This time, he had all the leverage. This time, he was the one who would be getting his whole way.

Even so, there was no reason to rub it in, to take what little dignity she had left; there was no need to do to her what she would have done to him. Without another word, he turned to go.

"You'd really destroy your own future just to get back at us?" his mom said from behind him. "You hate me that much?"

He stopped just long enough to answer the question. "I don't hate you at all," he said. "But you forced me to choose between myself and you. And I chose myself."

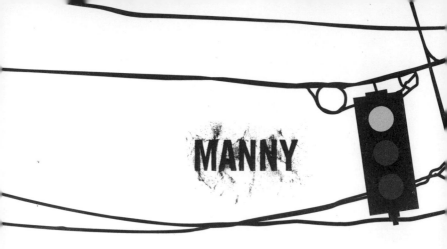

MANNY

Manny sat across from his dad at the kitchen table.

"Your parents were killed in a car accident when you were three years old," his dad said.

"I know," Manny said. "You told me this already."

His dad shook his head. "I didn't tell you the whole truth. I said you were home with a baby-sitter, but you weren't. You were with them in the car."

"A truck," Manny said without thinking. "We were hit by a truck."

His dad stared at him. "That's right. Do you remember the accident?"

Did Manny remember the accident? Or was he just remembering his last nightmare, where he'd come up from out of the cave-in and been creamed by the front of a truck?

"My nightmares!" Manny said suddenly. "The

accident is what my nightmares are all about!" The truck. The asteroid. The tidal wave. He thought about his other nightmares too—they all involved something huge slamming into him.

Then there was the smell of gasoline. That was part of all his recent nightmares as well. Was that another buried memory from the accident? Did the truck crash into their car, rupturing the gas tank, and had Manny, even as a three-year-old, somehow registered the smell?

"Glasses!" This time, Manny shouted.

His dad was confused. "What about them?"

"Did my biological father wear glasses?"

Manny's dad hesitated. "Yeah. I guess he did."

So, in the aftermath of the accident, Manny had somehow seen his dad's broken spectacles, and remembered. He must have seen the whole accident, but suppressed it. Manny still had no conscious memory of the event itself, not even fleeting images. But the memories were in his head somewhere, pushed deep into the Mariana Trench of his subconscious, and now images from those memories were bubbling upward, resurfacing in the form of nightmares.

So was that it? Had Manny solved the Mystery of the Recurring Nightmares? Would they finally go away for good?

His dad didn't say anything, just looked down at the table.

"Why didn't you tell me?" Manny asked.

"You had no memory," his dad said. "Not just of the accident. Of your parents. The doctor said not to push things. That your memory might return someday. Or that because of your young age, you might never remember. He did tell me that you might have nightmares, but you never did. Not until just these past few months."

"No," Manny said. "I mean, why didn't you tell me all this yesterday? You said that when my parents were killed, I was home with a baby-sitter."

"Downtown," his dad said. "At the intersection of Grand and Humble. That's where the accident was. It was a miracle you weren't killed too. A damn miracle."

That's interesting, Manny wanted to say. But it isn't the answer to the question I asked.

"Dad?" Manny said.

Suddenly his dad stood up and turned away, toward the stove. A second later, the teakettle on that stove began to whistle, almost as if his dad had somehow known it was going to happen.

His dad reached for the kettle and started pouring the boiling water into a teapot.

"Dad," Manny said, more forcefully.

"Damn!" his dad said. He'd burned his hand from a splash of hot water.

"Dad! Answer me!"

His dad put the kettle back on the stove and swung toward the sink. He turned the cold water on full blast and plunged his hand under it. He was still facing away from Manny, so it took a second for Manny to realize that his dad was crying.

"Dad?"

He didn't answer. Manny wasn't sure if his dad could hear him over the splashing of the water, so he stood up and walked to the sink. His dad's body was shaking, like he was in the middle of an earthquake, but one centered on him alone.

"Dad?" he repeated.

His dad turned and buried his face in Manny's chest. "Manny, I'm sorry! I'm really, really sorry!"

He let his dad hold him, cry on his shoulder. But tears or no tears, his dad had promised him answers, and Manny was determined to get them.

He gripped his dad by the shoulders and pushed him away; for the first time that Manny could remember, his dad looked old, broken. He could see the angry red welt on his dad's hand from where he'd spilled the hot water. It looked a little like a heart—or maybe the Batman logo.

"Dad?" Manny said. "Why are you sorry? For not telling me the truth? It's okay, all right?"

His dad shook his head and started to turn away, but stopped himself. "It's not that. I'm sorry for that too. But I'm more sorry for the accident. You almost died!"

"But that wasn't your fault. It's not like you were driving the truck that hit us." Manny froze. "Wait. Dad, you *weren't* driving that truck, were you?" Could it be? Distraught truck driver adopts the orphaned child of the parents he killed?

His dad dried his hand on a nearby towel. "No, that's the one thing I didn't do."

"Then what? Why are you sorry about the accident? You weren't to blame. You didn't even know me then. You hadn't adopted me yet."

His dad didn't answer. Manny was certain his dad was about to start crying again, so he reached out a hand and directed him back to the table. "Sit down, Dad. Tell me what happened."

His dad sat. Manny turned off the faucet. After the sound of splashing water, the silence was deafening.

"I did know you," his dad said softly, before Manny had even had a chance to sit.

"What?" Manny said.

"I knew you," his dad said. "Before the accident. Of course I did. I was your father."

Wordlessly, Manny took the seat opposite his dad.

"You're my son, Manny. My *biological* son. Those parents who were killed in the car accident at Grand and Humble? They adopted you from me. When you were nine months old. After they were killed, I adopted you back."

Manny listened, struggling to understand. It was like trying to make sense of a foreign language when he'd only studied it from books in a classroom—the words were coming too fast, too garbled. His dad was both his adoptive *and* his biological father? But that didn't make any sense.

"You had a mother, of course," his dad said. "My girlfriend—we weren't married. She did die, but not of skin cancer, and not when I told you. She left when you were two months old, and I never saw her again. She died a few years later, in a drug overdose. She was a drug addict." His dad wasn't on the verge of crying now. He was now completely without emotion. It was like Manny was talking to a robot.

"I decided to raise you myself," his dad went on. "A single father, that part was true. But I wasn't a very good father. And when you were nine months old, I lost custody."

"What?" Manny said. He had to choke out the word.

"There was an accident, and you almost died. It was my fault. I should have been watching you more closely." So Manny had almost died twice—once in the car with his adoptive parents and once even earlier, when he'd had some kind of accident with his dad?

"The state took you away from me," his dad was saying. "They gave you to different parents. It almost killed me. I was depressed, so I went out and did a lot of really stupid things. And I destroyed everything that had anything to do with you, every toy, every picture. I couldn't bear to be reminded."

"All except for the jack-in-the-box," Manny whispered.

His dad nodded. "A gift from my sister. You loved it so much—it was your favorite toy—I couldn't bear to throw it away.

"About two years later," his dad said, "your new parents were killed in that car accident. A complete fluke. But I saw my opportunity. I petitioned the court. It took a while, but I convinced them I could raise you right this time. And finally they awarded me custody again. At this point, I had no legal rights to you, so I had to adopt my own son."

Manny had questions, lots of them. But he couldn't

get them out. He still didn't speak the language.

"For a year or so," his dad said, "we stayed in the town where we'd lived before I lost you. And it was too much. Everyone was watching me, assuming I'd screw up again. I didn't want you growing up with a loser for a dad. And so we left. We moved here, to the big city, where you'd lived with your adoptive parents. No one knew us here. That was the real reason we left, not what I told you yesterday, about the prejudice from my being a single father. It was because of me, because I was ashamed of what I'd done. But I finally did turn my life around." He looked down at the burn on his hand. "I don't know what I would've done if I hadn't gotten you back in my life."

There was silence when his dad stopped talking, but Manny imagined he could still hear the rushing of water in the sink.

"Why didn't you ever tell me all this?" Manny said at last.

His dad shifted in his chair, back and forth, like he was struggling to get up but couldn't, like he was tied there with ropes. "I'd planned to," he said. "But after a while, I stopped thinking about it. It was a part of my life I wanted to forget. I was a different person then. I didn't want you to know that old person. I told myself there wasn't any reason for you to know. Then you started having those nightmares. A few weeks ago, that day at breakfast, I finally realized what they meant. You were starting to remember." Suddenly Manny's dad began to sob. It was like someone had flipped a switch and turned the emotion back on. "I'm sorry!" his dad said. "I'm so sorry!"

Manny reached out a hand. "Dad, it's okay. *I'm* okay. It's over now."

"No!" His dad looked up with haunted eyes. "Don't forgive me! I did something unforgivable— the one thing a parent *can't* do! I put the life of my child at risk. Twice! First when I got drunk and left you alone in that bathtub and you almost drowned, then again when you were riding in the car with your adoptive parents. You wouldn't have been there if it hadn't been for me. I don't want to be forgiven for that! I *can't* be."

A bathtub? Manny thought to himself. That was the accident his dad had caused when Manny was a baby—his dad had gotten drunk and left him unattended in a bathtub? Was that why his dad was so afraid of his ever going swimming, why he'd never let Manny take swimming lessons? Even after all these years, was he still afraid that Manny was going to drown?

His dad had been living in his own private hell for

years, Manny thought. Not because of the things he had done. Because of how much he loved Manny. A truly bad parent would have made the same mistakes, but then wouldn't have thought twice about them afterward—probably would have somehow even blamed them on the kid. Not so his dad. His dad was in agony.

"Dad?" Manny said.

"I mean it!" his dad said. "I don't want your forgiveness!"

"Who says I'm forgiving you?" said Manny with mock indignation. "You did a really stupid thing when I was nine months old, and there's no taking that back." Manny gave his dad the fisheye. "And, for the record, I'm not forgiving you for lying about all this either!" His dad looked up, unsure. "But as far as I can remember," Manny went on, "those are the only two bad things you've done in the seventeen years you've been my father. And when everything is said and done, you still come out ahead. I wouldn't want anyone else for a father."

His dad started to speak again, but stopped himself this time. A smile tickled his lips.

"What?" Manny said.

"Do you know why I first started calling you by your nickname?"

"'Manny'? No."

"Because I used to call you 'my little man.' I told myself that you were like a little man, strong and stoic and unfeeling. I think I wanted it to be true because of all you'd gone through. But it wasn't true. You were always so sensitive. You were like an emotional Geiger counter, able to pick up the tiniest flicker of emotion in any room. It was stupid of me to think you wouldn't figure all this out sooner or later.

"But the thing is," his dad went on, "it ended up being a good nickname for you anyway. You're a good man, Manny. The best man I know. You're someone I'm proud to call my son. So I don't care that no one ever calls you by your real name. You were named after my father, by the way. But I suppose that's one more thing I wanted to forget."

"Tell me about my adoptive parents," Manny said.

"It was my sister and her husband," his dad said. "She and I never got along. When you almost died in that bathtub, they petitioned the court, probably more out of spite than anything. It was . . . complicated. The husband was in politics—a real up-and-comer, or so they said. Everyone said he was destined for big things. Who knows? Maybe, if they'd lived, you'd be the son of the president right now."

Manny rolled his eyes. "No, thanks." He didn't

want to dwell on the past, at least not right now. But there was one thing he wanted to know. "What were their names? Your sister and her husband."

"Your adoptive parents?" he said. "Victoria and Lawrence Chesterton. So if that accident at Grand and Humble had never happened and your adoptive parents had lived, right now your name would be Harlan Chesterton."

HARLAN AND MANNY

The light turned green, and a red 360 Modena Ferrari peeled out right in front of Harlan. He knew he'd been to this intersection before; he just couldn't think when. It was the corner of Grand and Humble, and Harlan was standing by the crosswalk waiting for the light to change. He'd come downtown on a Saturday to walk around a bit, and to maybe pick out a new Speedo at the swim shop up the street.

Then it hit him. This was the exact spot where he'd almost been hit by that bus the night of the Bittle Society dinner. The streets had been so foggy then that he'd stepped right out into its path. Things sure looked different in the daylight.

A lot had changed since that night. Or maybe just one thing: he'd finally stood up to his mom. It was only one change, but it was a doozy. It meant that he was in control of his life now; he was sitting behind the wheel. So it made sense that there wasn't any fog on these downtown streets now, that everything was bright and clear and dazzling—the fog had been swept out of his life as well. He didn't need Marilyn Swan after all, because he knew any dark forces were well and truly gone.

Well, most of them, anyway. True, he wouldn't have his mom telling him what to do anymore. But there was still the small matter of figuring out what *he* wanted to do.

Oh, that, he thought to himself.

Yeah, that.

The light changed to "Walk," and Harlan moved to cross the street. But as he did, he felt someone tapping on his shoulder.

It was Elsa, that girl from school. She was the first person he'd told about his premonitions—that afternoon in the school theater after class.

"Oh!" Harlan said. "Hey!" He stopped right there on the corner, letting the pedestrians headed for the crosswalk pass by them on either side.

I thought it was you! she signed excitedly. *What are you doing downtown?*

He started signing to her. *Just wandering.* The

light changed to "Don't Walk," but that was okay.

How's it going? she asked. He knew she meant with the premonitions.

To tell you the truth, he said, *it's going great. You were right, you know. I just needed a little more control.* Harlan had signed with lots of deaf people before—the impaired kids he worked with at the YMCA, and elsewhere. But it had never felt this effortless. With Elsa, it was almost like they had their own private language.

Yeah? Elsa signed. *That's fantastic!*

Harlan smiled. *How about you? Did you ever ask that guy out? The one you had a crush on?*

What? Elsa said. *Oh, no. Not yet.* She didn't grimace or mug, the way Harlan would have expected her to. She blushed, flustered by the question.

And in a flash, Harlan knew: it was him. *He* was the guy Elsa had the crush on. Duh! It was so obvious! How could he have not seen it that day in the theater?

Out on the street, the light changed, and a car laid on the horn for a slow-moving pedestrian.

What about you? Elsa signed. *Did you ever break up with Amber?*

Actually, she broke up with me, Harlan said. *Through e-mail.* It was true. She'd sent him a breakup e-mail that was all of four words long: "Let's break up, k?" And that was fine with Harlan.

So what are you doing downtown? he asked.

Actually, I'm scouting locations for this movie I'm working on.

Really? What's it about?

She slouched. *Oh, nothing. It's stupid. It's just this dumb video.*

Come on! he said.

Well, it's called Im-Patient. *It's about a deaf guy who waits so long at his doctor's office that he finally goes berserk. He destroys the office, then goes running through the streets screaming.*

Harlan laughed. *Hey, that sounds great! Let me know if you need any help.*

Seriously? she asked.

Sure, why not!

She straightened a bit. *As a matter of fact, I do need an actor. And it's the lead!*

Really? The patient? It took a second for Harlan to imagine himself as an actual actor. But to his surprise, the idea excited him.

"Hey," said a voice behind Harlan. "You crossing or not?"

Harlan turned. It was a guy in a wheelchair trying to cross the street, but Harlan was standing in front of the ramp. Across the street, the signal had changed to "Walk" again.

"Hey, man, sorry," Harlan said, stepping out of the way. He looked at Elsa again. *Well*, he signed, *I should probably . . .*

You busy now? Elsa signed quickly.

No. Why?

Maybe we could get a cup of coffee or something. She quickly added, *We could talk about the role?*

Harlan smiled. Was she asking him out? Well, why not? Hadn't he encouraged her to ask out the guy she had a crush on? And why shouldn't he go? She was smart and funny. Even if it turned out there wasn't any chemistry there, at least he might make another friend.

He bowed gallantly. *I'm all yours.*

And with that, Elsa blushed and turned away from the crosswalk, leading him on down the sidewalk.

The red car right in front of Manny screeched as it took off from the intersection. He didn't know what kind of car it was—a Ferrari?—but he knew it was expensive (and that the driver was almost certainly an asshole). On the far side of the crosswalk, the signal now read "Don't Walk"—perfectly in focus,

Manny noticed; his eyes were never out of focus these days, and his headaches were gone too. But he wasn't there waiting to cross the street. He'd come here, to the corner of Grand and Humble, to see the place where his adoptive parents had been killed.

This was where it had happened: where he'd been riding in a car with his onetime parents and they'd been hit by that truck. They'd died, but he'd lived. So it was also the spot where his life had peeled off in a completely different direction.

What would have happened if they hadn't died, these parents Manny had never met—who, before a few days ago, he hadn't even known existed? What would his life be like now if that accident hadn't occurred—if the truck had managed to slam on its brakes or if, at the last second, his parents had somehow happened to swerve out of the way?

Across the street, the signal changed back to "Walk," but Manny didn't move. He couldn't, not just yet. He saw pedestrians surge by on either side of him, caught a couple of people glancing back at him standing there, unmoving, on the sidewalk, their faces flickering with glimmers of confusion or annoyance.

Manny knew his life would be different if his adoptive parents had lived, but *how* different? He might still live in the same city, but would he go to the same high school? Would Elsa be his best friend? And would *he* be different? Having been shaped by an entirely different set of circumstances from age three until today, would he have any of the same interests, the same sensibilities? Would he even be recognizable as the same person?

Manny couldn't help but wonder which life would be "better." The way things had worked out, it almost seemed that even though his life had been knocked off course by his dad's screwup with the bathtub, things had eventually righted themselves and he'd ended up back where he was supposed to be all along—with his dad. But what if it was the other way around? What if it was the incident in the bathtub that had put his life on the "right" road with his new parents and the death of those parents had pushed him off-track again?

On the other side of the crosswalk, the light changed back to "Don't Walk." But the words were still flashing, so a couple of straggling pedestrians dashed out into the street in an effort to beat the light. Some ten seconds later, an Asian teenager sauntered into the crosswalk, indifferent to—or maybe taking secret satisfaction in—the fact that he was going to hold up traffic.

Manny started laughing. The teenager glanced back at him, scowling, thinking Manny was laughing at him. But it was something else that had made him laugh—a moment of absolute focus.

His life wasn't about any *two* directions! Sure, the thing with the bathtub and the accident here at Grand and Humble had changed the course of his life. But something probably happened every day, maybe even every hour, that changed the direction of his life, turning him one way or another. Some of these events Manny might control, but most of them he didn't; most of them were the result of random chance—or at least forces way beyond *his* control. As for all those other lives he never lived, well, some really might have been "better" than the one he was experiencing now. But Manny had no way of comparing! Because once he took a step—or was pushed—in any one direction, all those other lives faded into the gloom. All that ever existed was the here and now. The only choice Manny had was making the best of that.

"Hey," said a voice behind him. "You crossing or not?"

"Huh?" Manny said, jumping a little. There was a guy in a wheelchair just behind him. The signal had changed to "Walk" again, but Manny was blocking the ramp into the street. "Oh," he said, embarrassed. "Sorry."

And with that, Manny stepped forward into the crosswalk and continued on to the opposite side of the street.

ACKNOWLEDGMENTS

A special thanks to Jeff Graham, Marshall Moore, Ron Podmore, and Becky Wojahn for taking the time to help me better understand the world of the Deaf.